You shall serve me, human. Step forward and hold out your left hand.

Athu did so, and gasped suddenly as a sharp pain stung him—as if his left wrist had been cut with a sharp knife. He could feel blood rilling warmly down his upraised forearm, dripping off his elbow.

Hold out your hand.

Again he obeyed, the blood from his cut wrist dripping onto the cave floor.

You will sleep now, the weird voice droned on. *Your blood will bring me strength, and my strength will bring you healing. Your soul is mine forever. . .*

RED SONJA

3

WHEN HELL LAUGHS

DAVID C. SMITH & RICHARD L. TIERNEY

SF
ace books
A Division of Charter Communications Inc.
A GROSSET & DUNLAP COMPANY
51 Madison Avenue
New York, New York 10010

RED SONJA #3: WHEN HELL LAUGHS
Copyright © 1982 by Glenn Lord

An ACE Book

First Ace printing: June 1982
Published Simultaneously in Canada

2 4 6 8 0 9 7 5 3 1
Manufactured in the United States of America

"Know also, O prince, that in those selfsame days that Conan the Cimmerian did stalk the Hyborian Kingdoms, one of the few swords worthy to cross with his was that of Red Sonja, warrior-woman out of majestic Hyrkania. Forced to flee her homeland because she spurned the advances of a king and slew him instead, she rode west across the Turanian Steppes and into the shadowed mists of legendry."
—*The Nemedian Chronicles*

Agonies are one of my changes of garments.
—Whitman

Chapter 1

The man stumbled painfully through the shadows of the night-darkened forest. The night was warm, and mosquitoes sang in a cloud about him, attracted by the drying blood of his recent wounds. He paid them no heed. His pain was too great to allow him to notice the bites of a few insects, and even greater than the ache of his physical wounds was the pain of the hatred and humiliation that burned within him.

Hate, humiliation and purpose. Though the blackness beneath the forest canopy was almost utter, the man limped on, unhesitating, as if guided by some unnatural sixth sense.

But, then, he had come this way many times. For he alone of all who dwelt upon this accursed prison-isle had dared to seek out this region. He alone had heard of its secret . . .

Suddenly he emerged from the forest into a large clearing. The sound of a waterfall, heard but dimly before, was now loud in his ears. Under the light of the full moon he could see the water spilling, a narrow band from the lip of a low cliff, to thunder into a pool below. A brief thrill of fear passed through him, despite the hate and the pain and his previous knowledge of the place. The face of the cliff bore an uncanny resemblance to the face of a skull.

Swordskull, they called it, and for centuries beyond

memory it had been a place of evil legendry, so that now the whole southwest quarter of Os Harku was shunned because of it. Doubtless, too, that was why the entire island of Os Harku had originally been made a place of banishment for criminals.

The man stood silently, hesitating, while the dark blood dried on his limbs. He was a rather short man, yet stocky and powerfully built. His right hand hung limply, awkwardly; he knew it was at least sprained, if not broken. Blood dripped from his thick black beard, for he had lost several teeth. Yet for the moment, fear made him forget his pain. It was uncanny, the way those caves and ledges resembled the eyes, nose and lineaments of a skull, how those great boulders down by the pool resembled its teeth. The narrow waterfall, a silver ribbon in the moonlight, spilled over the right eye from a notch in the rounded brink of the cliff—a notch like that from a great sword-stroke.

Perhaps another time . . .

Yet even as the thought crossed his mind, he knew it was now or never. Tonight happened to be the full moon nearest the summer solstice—a night of great sorcerous potency. Perhaps the monstrous Primal Gods had willed it so—had guided the events leading up to his humiliation.

His lips drew back in a snarl at the remembrance of that humiliation; his dark eyes glinted with hatred under the shining moon. Hesitating no longer, he advanced to the pool's edge and raised high his arms.

"Ordru!" he cried out in a deep, powerful voice. *"Ordru—I come!"*

Then he dove into the pool, hearing the thunder of the water as he swam beneath the surface. His right hand pained him severely with each stroke, yet he kept doggedly on. Now he was at the base of the boulders, feeling for the tunnel he knew was there. He found it, and swam inward.

The sound of water diminished. Now a new fear

began to creep over the man as he groped forward, for he had never been beyond this point before. Suppose there was no air-space above—or suppose some guardian lurked here . . .

But even as these fears grew within him, he felt the roof of the tunnel slope upward, and in another moment his head emerged above the water's surface. An instant later he felt what seemed to be a low ledge, and climbed upon it. For a time he crouched there, breathing as quietly as he could, listening.

He knew this place, and knew that his was the first human foot to tread here since the great cataclysm that had destroyed the Primal Lands. He knew, too, that the cliff's resemblance to a skull was deliberate. The darkness and the silence were absolute; he would have given much for a torch, yet knew that one would seal his death. Light had never been allowed in this place, not since the pre-human lords of men had built it. Here, light was blasphemy.

The man slowly stood up, and his voice trembled slightly as he muttered: "Ordru . . ."

Silence.

Then, he felt a faint vibration—a low-pitched tremor, though the man could not tell whether it was in the air, the rock or his flesh. Gradually it grew in intensity.

Who comes?

The voice, if such it was, seemed to tremble within the bones of his skull, as if it vibrated from the very fabric of space.

Who comes to the fane of Ordru?

"I—I am Athu," the man stammered, "—a sorcerer of Shem, now banished to this prison-isle. I seek your aid, O Ordru, and offer you my service in return."

Again there was silence. The man called Athu felt the air prickle on the back of his neck. Though there was no sound, he somehow sensed something monstrous and alien stirring in the blackness—something he knew had not stirred for thousands of years.

This isle? the voice said finally after a long pause. *My temple was established upon a great eminence of land, far from water.*

"Aye—by your worshipers, after they fled the foundering of the Primal Continent and came here. That was long ago. Few humans know now of your worship, Great Ordru, save a handful of sages and sorcerers learned in the lore of Acheron and Atlantis. I read of it many years ago—in *The Book of Wisdom* by Damar Eltek, of Sei."

Sei—that was a city of Neria, a nation of the Primal Continent. But Atlantis—Acheron—these names I know not.

"You have slept long, O Ordru," said Athu. "These lands, now of ancient memory, were yet unborn when cataclysm destroyed the nations you knew. Atlantis has sunk beneath the ocean, even as did the Primal Land, and Acheron fell many centuries ago. Now the Hyborian nations rule the earth, dominating the land of Shem where my people dwell.

"Long have I fought these Hyborians with sorcery and subterfuge, O Ordru—first in the courts of Koth, that land which holds my own in subjugation, and finally in Aquilonia itself, mightiest of all the nations. Great were the ills I helped to bring upon them by sorcery and intrigue—war, sicknesses and crop-failures—yet never was my power more than a pin-prick to their arrogant empire. And at last I was discovered, convicted of sorcery and sent to this barbaric prison isle to die. That was many months ago.

"Therefore I am here, O Ordru—offering you my service."

Again there was silence for a space.

You would have vengeance. I read it in your soul.

"Vengeance!" muttered Athu; then, more vehemently, "Aye—vengeance on the Kothians who sacked my homeland—on the Aquilonians who banished me to this prison-isle—but above all, on the barbarian who tonight laid violent hands on me, reviled me, humiliated me—!"

The Shemite's voice choked off in the intensity of his rage. Had there been any light in that place, his eyes would have reflected a glare of madness.

You shall serve me, human. Step forward, and hold out your left hand.

Athu took a deep breath and did so, one step, two . . .

Suddenly he gasped as a sharp pain stung him—as if his left wrist had been cut with a sharp knife. Involuntarily he drew back. He could feel blood rilling warmly down his upraised forearm, dripping off his elbow.

Hold out your hand.

He forced himself to do so. For a moment it sounded like the blood from his cut wrist was dripping into a shallow container. Then he began to see the faintest tinge of a red glow forming near the floor, outlining the interior of a small, square receptacle. A ringing began to grow in his ears.

You will sleep now, the weird voice droned on. *Your blood will bring me strength, and my strength will bring you healing. Your soul is mine forever. When you awaken you will have new powers and your body will be renewed. And one day, you will have a body greater than any human one, the better to serve me—and at the last, to serve my Master.*

Athu had sunk to his knees; the ringing in his ears was very loud now. The redness in the square container seemed brighter, and by its glow . . . was it his dizziness, or a swarm of red eyes . . .?

"Your Master," he muttered weakly. "I know his name—aye, Arkatu, that primal god who fled the foundering First Lands."

For an instant the rock floor seemed to shudder, but whether or not this was due to his growing dizziness, Athu could not tell.

Speak not again His name, until the time when you shall with sorcery draw new souls to my feast and His, said the voice of Ordru. *Sleep now, and I will renew your strength,*

*that you may work to gather even greater strength unto
me. I will grant you vengeance upon your enemies, that in
the fullness of time I may work my far greater vengeance.*

"I hear, O Ordru," muttered the Shemite wizard as
his mind slowly dissolved into unconsciousness. "Vengeance—vengeance . . ."

Urdus, the giant red-maned Vanir, sat with his tribe on
the shelf of rock that rose above the treetops of the isle.
Absently he fingered the haft of his knife. Evening was
coming, warm and muggy. Urdus' band of sixty-odd
comrades crowded around fires, chewing on roast fowl
and fruit and arguing over portions of sour wine which
they had themselves made from wild grapes. Urdus was
in a foul mood. His blackness had come to visit him
again—his longing to be gone from this damned isle and
return to Aquilonia and kill the scoundrel who had banished him.

The island was situated in the middle of the wide
Shirki River. If it had ever been dubbed with an official
name, that was long ago forgotten by the Aquilonian
scribes, for now it was known all along the coast by its
most common and descriptive appellation: *Os Harku,*
the Isle of Ill Harbor—or, more simply, the Isle. It was
not visited by pleasure ships or cruising trade vessels,
but galleasses from the Aquilonian forts on the shore
patrolled the waters about it. For Os Harku was populated, not by voluntary settlers or emigrants, but by
criminals.

Murders, political rebels, men and women with personal histories steeped in crime and violence, necessarily
or expediently banished from home soil to the forests
and cliffs and swamps of the Isle—such were the five or
six hundred criminals living upon Os Harku. Neither the
Aquilonian throne nor the border forts kept any census.
That would have been useless, as the population rose
and fell daily, depending upon the tempers of its exiles
and the vicissitudes of their daily struggles. Once a

month an Aquilonian galley, crowded with swordsmen and archers of the state army, would drop anchor at the shore of the Isle and ferry across the latest troop of ostracized unwanteds. From time to time a sally of ambitious criminals would attack the longboats in a desperate attempt for freedom. Such attempts had always failed. The archers, poised, ready and eager for target practice, would unleash their arrows and feather as many of the rogues as they could, till the surviving criminals would howl in rage and pain and retreat to the protection of the thick foliage.

A few hardy souls had, however, escaped from the Isle. This was known. Accident or design or fate had guided them safely across the river and onto home soil. The throne, disturbed by such escapades, had always thereafter increased the patrols for a time and resigned the current commandants to replace them with fresher men, vigilant and eager for advancement. In any event, escapees usually returned to their old haunts—if they were fortunate enough to survive life in the wild—where they were almost always rediscovered and then executed.

The criminals of the Isle were a hard lot, and their life was as difficult and tempestuous and sordid as the struggle ever has been for society's outcasts. Upon Os Harku, strength, quickness, and temper created the hierarchy. Men far outnumbered the women, and only the fiercest and most brutal of men had gained the women—if the women allowed themselves to be had, for more than one renegade had screamed out in the night and run weeping through the forest, hugging his bloody trousers, after trying to force his attentions upon some woman in a less than amorous mood.

Tribes had formed upon the island, and territory. Certain stretches of Os Harku were but swampland, and here lived the outcasts of the outcast—those who, intimidated and fearful for their lives, or for other reasons known only to themselves, inhabited the wastelands in solitude, apart from their comrades. Other portions of the island offered small pools or fresh streams, and the protection of deep woods; and still other territories evolved upon the high cliffs, the rocky faces being pocked with shallow caves both defensible and advantageous for perception. The woods and the cliffs were marked off by rude boundaries: northeast of the Great Oak was the land of Obgur and his tribe; Central Lake belonged to Shihur the Demoness, and her band. Newcomers to the island not only had to forage for themselves and defend themselves against attack from members of the various tribes, but also to seek inclusion into one or another of the territories. Deftness with knife, sword or fists decided one's rank in the hierarchy.

The cliffs which guarded Old Lake and the surrounding forest of wild apple trees and berry thorns belonged to Urdus, the brawny Vanir, half a head taller than most big men, who swore he had spent half his life upon the Isle and had never lost a hand-to-hand with anyone there. The Vanir commanded a certain amount of respect among the veterans of Os Harku; and in the rude society which had developed under his hand, men at odds with one another had often taken their grievances to him for arbitration rather than decide them bloodily in the forest. Urdus was not old—he was barely past thirty-three summers, and he had remained trim and muscular and quick. Yet, for all that he had spent half his years upon the Isle, never had he given up the ambition to one day return to Aquilonia and slay a certain nobleman in the capital—the man who had had him sent to Os Harku.

But Urdus was also patient, with the patience of the intelligent and the conniving. Several times Urdus had broached his escape to comrades, then feigned illness as the time approached; thus, when the others inevitably attempted their escape without him, he was able to study the practical applications of his plottings. Once he had planned escape through the southwestern swamps; the

death-screams of his friends that night had warned
Urdus against that route. Another time he had considered building a raft and sailing across to the eastern
shore; but the laboriousness of that conveyance had led
to its capture by the trim Aquilonian galleasses.

Urdus was no fool. Yet, plans of escape—and revenge
—still whispered in the caverns of his mind.

Sitting on his rock ledge, playing with the knife in his
hand, he burped and scowled and stared upon his crew
with vulture-eyes. Beside him sat Aleil, the slatternly
woman who had decided to be Urdus' mate. But this
night her presence suffocated the giant Vanir. He knew
that her temperament was as his own—morose one moment, brilliant the next, with the untrusting selfishness
the gods give to some at birth. Aleil was no comfort to
him, no friend with whom to muse or share confidences.

For that matter, no one was a friend; no one was
trustworthy.

Urdus listened to the calls of the night birds, and he
wondered that they stayed on Os Harku, when they
could soar easily over the waters and alight in freedom
on shore.

But they were birds, with wings. Any land on earth
was free to them, so long as they remained out of range
of the bolt and the arrow. They stayed because they were
birds, and stupid; Urdus stayed because he had never
known of a man who could grow wings and fly.

"Did you see the galleass today?" asked one lean,
bronze skinned rogue, hunched before a fire and chewing carefully at the roasted thigh of a water-rodent.

Heads nodded; voices grunted in the shimmering firelight.

"Not as many men as usual," replied one.

"If it's that small a force tomorrow, we might swim
out and take our chances," commented another.

"Fools!" snorted a third. "They're waiting for us.
Can you walk on the water? Is there a tree anywhere tall
enough to fell and use as a bridge? It'll take stealth and

luck to get us off this island."

"And why leave?" said another, an old man who lived simply by the protection of his more brawny fellows. They called him Veljo, the old man, though he had been born with a different name. "Our life here is the same as at home. It's all a bother, no matter where you live, or how."

Urdus grunted with impatience. Veljo looked up at him and their eyes met—the old man's bright with the firelight, Urdus' shadowed like deep holes, sullen and masked.

"You enjoy your cage?" Urdus asked.

"Where is the cage, Urdus?" said Veljo. "Perhaps we are free, and those on the mainland are caged. There are no prison bars. We pay no taxes. We forage freely for food, or grow it like any gardener."

A few nearby, overhearing, laughed at Veljo. It seemed obvious that his years upon the Isle had shrivelled his brain.

"Freedom is freedom," Veljo said, hunching forward and grabbing a rodent-thigh from the spit. "We are free here to do as we please."

"Except return to the mainland," said a man close to him.

Veljo shrugged. He stood up, munching on the greasy thigh, and walked off into the darkness.

"Fool," Urdus muttered.

"Leave him to his birds and flowers," said another man. "The spark has gone out of him. The swamp-mists have rotted his brain."

Urdus shifted his position. "Throw me some meat, Betos," he growled.

The man nodded, smiling grimly. His gnarled left hand, missing two fingers, plucked a leg from the spit and tossed it steaming through the air. Urdus caught it and brought it to his mouth in one motion.

Aleil nudged closer to the giant Vanir and looked up at him, but Urdus paid her no mind.

Footsteps sounded on the brittle mulch just beyond the range of the fires. Urdus looked up, only mildly curious. A few faces at the fire turned around, some already guessing who the intruder must be. One man, seated on a rock and burnishing his boots with grease-drippings collected from supper, moved aside to let the newcomer approach.

It was Athu, the Shemite.

The few Shemites on the Isle were objects of scorn and derision, prejudice. Athu himself, the day before, had suffered a brutal humiliation at Urdus' hands for having dared to approach Aliel—as the bruises on his body still testified.

But Athu, as most there already knew, was more than a simple Shemite. He was a sorcerer—or so he claimed.

He took a seat on a warm log by one of the fires, not far from Urdus and Aleil. A number of rogues deliberately left, sensing impending trouble. Athu paid them no heed. He reached for a roasted breast of fowl and began to munch at it. His several strange amulets and chains jangled and clanked as he moved on his log.

Urdus studied the man minutely, as he often had before, with an impassive mixture of distaste and mistrust. A sorcerer, indeed. Urdus' sorcery lay in his sword, and he knew that the Shemite prattler could never hope to match that wizardry.

"You are thinking of escape," Athu said suddenly, speaking to Urdus but not looking at him, and never missing a bite or chew of his cooked fowl.

Aleil looked at Athu, then to Urdus.

"Am I?" Urdus' voice was as gruff and husky as the surrounding shadows. There was not enough humility in Athu's tone to suit him.

"I will aid you."

"Don't do me any favors, Shemite."

Athu smiled obscurely. "You believe my sorcery is a lie."

Urdus' teeth worked within his mouth as his anger

stirred. "I believe you'll be found dead one night if you keep joking about escape."

"Every day you think of escape," Athu replied. "Every day every damned soul on this isle dreams of escape. Their musings create a fog. I can hardly breathe, sometimes, trying to fight through the fog of your dreams."

"Don't *you* dream of escape?" Aleil asked him tersely.

Athu eyed her. "Aye—I do."

"Has it aught to do with that secret work of yours within the swamp?"

Athu paused in his eating. "And what do you know of what I do there?"

"Is it a sorcery to help you escape?"

"My plans for escape are very different from your lover's plans, O Aleil. If Urdus escaped tonight, he could leave me behind. My plans require no man's aid."

Urdus threw his stripped meat bone into the fire. "Careful, Shemite. Have you forgotten who's leader here? You try me, and this time I'll gut you."

Athu grinned. Uneasily, Urdus noticed a strange, new light in the man's eyes. The wizard not only seemed less injured than he should have been after the beating he had received from Urdus, he also seemed more confident than he should have.

"Why do you hate me, Urdus? After all, I intend to help you. Why *should* you hate me?"

Urdus sneered.

"Listen," Athu told him. "I have conjured a storm. It will arrive in a day or two—an immense storm. Such a tempest cannot be called with a snap of the fingers—but it will arrive. And by this storm, you may plan your escape."

Aleil leaned forward a bit, intrigued. All the men at the fire had turned toward the Shemite, their senses alert to talk of escape. Aleil's shimmering black eyes devoured Athu's broad features. "Is this true?"

"A day or two will prove the truth of what I say."

Aleil looked up at Urdus. "Whether he causes the

storm or not, Urdus, won't it give us a chance of escape?"

Urdus sniffed the air and looked up at the sky above the hilltop precipices. "There will be no storm."

"Have you magic to counter my own?" Athu asked casually.

Urdus glared at him. "The wind is low. The stars shine clear. The air is unscented. There will be no storm."

"It will storm in one day, no more than two. You have my word. I have done my magic." Finishing his supper, Athu stood up with a clanking and jangling of chains, amulets and bone necklaces; saying no more, he trod off towards the swamps.

Aleil turned to Urdus; as did all the faces ringing the campfires.

"What if—?" began Aleil.

Bur Urdus only grunted and pulled himself erect, to his full height, huge and awesome. "You lie, wizard!" he cried out through the night; his voice carried distinctly across the woods and down the slopes.

No sound answered him from the dark forest.

Disgusted, Urdus turned on his heel and went into his cave. Aleil, sensing his anger, did not follow.

The giant Vanir lay down on his cot of old grasses and animal skins.

What if—?

What if it stormed in a day or two?

Such a storm might, indeed, provide an avenue of escape. Yet . . .

Despite himself, Urdus began to picture it, and ponder it, and plan it.

What if . . .?

Far out on the waters of the broad Shirki River, a woman slept in her cabin on shipboard—and dreamed.

Her name was Red Sonja and she was a mercenary, a swordswoman. Seldom did she dream, but this night she tossed and turned in the grip of a familiar, recurring nightmare.

Flames—her home in distant Hyrkania, burning. Blood—her family slain. The lean, grinning, taunting face that had brought the fire and the blood—the captain of the soldiers who had killed her father and mother and brothers before her eyes—

The soldiers who had beaten her, humiliated her, raped her.

She tossed on her bed, whimpering. In her mind she was running through the Hyrkanian forest, her soul afire with a pain that submerged all her bodily hurts, still not fully comprehending what had happened to her. She had lost all but life, and could not bear the anguish of that life. She was hardly more than a girl; now she was suddenly alone in the forest, in the world—alone with a shock too great to comprehend, fearful of every shadow, fearful of pursuit . . .

She was among great stones—stones that might once have formed the walls of ancient, pre-Hyborian walls and temples, but now tumbled randomly, half-hidden by moss and grass and great tree roots. She had played here often as a child—

A voice! She looked up. Something towering, glowing—

"You have suffered deeply, Sonja. Know now that there is strength born in suffering."

A God? A vision?

"You may use your strength to make the world your home. You may become a wanderer, the equal of any man or woman you meet."

She sensed a sword in her hand—her father's sword. Suddenly she felt almost invincible.

"But first you must make a *vow* to me, Sonja. You must never allow yourself to be *loved* by another man, unless he has defeated you in fair battle—something *no* man is likely to do after this day."

Anger and vengeance-lust welled within her young heart.

"Yes! With all my heart—with all my *soul*—I do so *vow!*"

A sound in the brush—one of the mercenaries, coming after her. His panting, cold face appeared through the tangle of growth. He laughed.

She lifted her father's sword as if it weighed no more than a twig. The mercenary noticed. "Take care, wench."

"Pig! Tarim will *damn your soul!*"

She leapt at him. He drew blade and fought, but he was no match for her—for this girl who had scarcely lifted a sword in her life. Her skill was incredible. Fear grew in the mercenary's eyes.

She thrust savagely. Was it a move learned by watching her father and later practiced secretly? Or a skill given her by the strange vision?

The mercenary stood there, blood spouting from the great wound in his chest, too surprised to realize that he was already a slain man. He stared at Sonja a moment; then his knees buckled and he flopped face-down into the wet grass.

And Sonja felt—*exhilaration*.

Suddenly she sat up in the darkness. The soft rocking of the ship, the sound of wavelets against the hull, reminded her of where she was.

"Erlik!" she gasped. "Again, the dream!"

But although she tried to banish the vision from her mind and compose herself for sleep, she knew it was not just a nightmare.

It was also a memory.

Chapter 2

Sonja awoke to the roll of the ship. Despite her night-mare, and though she had slept lightly the rest of the night—as was her habit and instinct—she faced the new day refreshed and wholly invigorated. For a moment she lay in her berth, enjoying the softness of her cushions and blankets and the lazy warmth of the sun spilling through the port hole. It was not often that she was permitted the finer things in life, such as this private cabin aboard an Aquilonian barge or soft blankets and cushions—or even the simple security afforded by the lock on her cabin door.

No, it was not often that Red Sonja, the Hyrkanian warrior-woman, enjoyed such privileges. The soreness of her muscles, the remembrance of recent fatigue and the still-healing bruises and marks of skirmish reminded her of that.

Beginning to feel almost guilty at her new-found lux-ury, Sonja rose from her cot and stretched, yawned and shook her long, tousled mane of bright red hair. She was tall, as was natural with her race, and lithe and cleanly muscular, as befit a woman who was no more at home by the loom or the cooking pot than any sailor on board this barge. Her figure was trim—not delicate, yet quite enough of a woman's body to earn her masculine whistles, jibes and smiling stares wherever she went. Regarding herself in the small mirror which hung on the back of her cabin door, Sonja placed her hands on her hips and was neither pleased nor displeased with herself. Ample in the bosom—tight in the belly . . .

Mitra! she thought then, cursing herself. Had she been too long aboard this fat ship in the company of noblemen's wives and Aquilonian patricians?

"Am I a city woman?" she muttered self-derisively, "to measure myself in terms of shapliness and the whiteness of my teeth and the blush of my cheek?"

Sonja ducked her hands and face into the washing basin, liberally splashing herself and the cabin deck, laving the last of sleepiness from her. The water was cold and refreshing. She shook her hair again and wiped it with her wet hands, then once more looked at herself in the mirror and squinted at her high cheekbones and sapphire eyes. Suddenly she lunged forward in mock contest, brought up her arm with the fleetness of an eyeblink, and in an instant had skewered the door three times with the point of an imaginary blade.

So much for life's reflections, she thought.

Sonja dressed. Her clothing did nothing to hide her figure. She had chosen it for the freedom of movement it allowed her—or, so she often told herself. A brief halter of scale-mail about her shoulders and breasts, a short skirt of the same hanging to mid-thigh, boots of rugged Nemedian leather—this was her outfit. This, and her sword—the sword which had once been her father's of good Hyrkanian steel, and tempered by Sonja in the blood of a thousand combats. She wore knives, too, strapped to her thighs.

Dressed, Sonja regarded herself once more in her mirror, then slid free her blade with the speed of a gasp and brought it up, shimmering in the dawnlight, and lunged forward—all in one graceful, unified motion betraying no waste, no uncertainty—bringing the point to just a hair's breadth from the surface of the mirror.

Smiling at herself, she sheathed the sword with a hiss

and a clank, unlocked her door and stepped out into the gallery.

She mounted the stairs to the waist. Tio, the master of the *Niros,* was coming down; he smiled at Sonja, and his gaze lingered.

"Breakfast awaits," he commented, pausing. "You're eating on deck, in the sunshine."

Sonja nodded.

Tio flashed a second smile and saluted Sonja, then made his way down into the gallery, his bulk heaving from side to side on sturdy legs with every rock of the ship.

Sonja looked after him. She wasn't quite sure how to take Tio's salutes. Bravado, or mock deference to her scant armor? She stepped up onto the deck.

When she had originally signed aboard as passenger on the *Niros,* Sonja had indulged herself with the idea that travelling down the Shirki River with a boatload of Aquilonian nobles and respectables would amuse her, and feed her curiosity. She—a warrior, a horsewoman, a sword-adept, sometimes an outcast, always a player with Fate and a challenger of Destiny—sharing the same boards as the soft, pale women of gentry and their soft, pale men of politics, the hierophants of councils and the hypocritical guardians of social law? It might be interesting.

Her curiosity had been sated the first hour out; and since then Sonja, in her turn, had been the unending focus of the curiosity of all others on board. Not that all the passengers on the *Niros* were patrician; anyone who could pay fare was accepted for the ride, and many on the barge were simple merchants, some wealthier than others, and bankers, and men of even lower social caste, travelling down river for one reason or other of their own. Yet all these, of course, were recognized as types by one another and taken for what they were. But Sonja. . .

Red Sonja, who didn't use make-up or dress her hair,

who swore and cursed like a barracks-trooper, who wore armor and bore a sword like a mercenary soldier. . .

Yet, a young woman possessed of natural presence and personality. A young woman of great beauty, which fact delighted the men.

And—a fact which delighted them even more—a young woman who, in her barbarous accent, cut right to the core of any argument, practiced no patience with any of the niceties and useless extravagances of polite conversation. A young woman who with disdain always gave back in equal measure what she got from the boring, languid matriarchs and matrons of Aquilonia's finer families.

A long dining table had been set up in the waist and the thirty-odd passengers of the *Niros* sat at breakfast, served by slaves. According to unspoken convention all the members of gentry had seated themselves at the upper end of the table while the merchants and bankers had accepted positions farther down, more or less according to social hierarchy. Sonja found this vastly amusing. Not once on this voyage had she sat beside a banker or merchant or travelling barber; a certain nobleman had always managed to save her a chair beside him, at the upper end of the social line.

Lord Sir Desmos, a man highly favored by the Aquilonian court, a legal counsellor and defender of the state, rose to his feet upon seeing Sonja. Smiling to her, he held up his hand and indicated her chair.

Sonja strode to the table. A few matrons side-glanced, then lifted their beaks to the air, while their husbands watched with lingering delight. Sonja, however, kept Sir Desmos waiting, for as she came up to the table she paused to whisper a salty jibe into the ear of some earthy fellow; and he, in turn, guffawed and slapped her on the behind as she went past. It was a ritual they went through every day. Sonja did not know the man's name; if he knew hers, he never spoke it. They never conversed otherwise during the cruise; they seldom passed each other, in fact, and Sonja had learned that the rogue spent most of his time with the pilots of the barge, mingling little with any others. Either he preferred his own kind, or harbored a romance for the sea—or the Shirki River. However, he'd once dropped a comment in Sonja's direction, she had retorted in kind, and their morning ritual had flowered.

Now Sonja took her chair beside Sir Desmos. He waited for her to be seated, offering her scented, courtly platitudes.

"A bright good morning to you, my dear Sonja! And it's a morning almost worthy to match you, for truly you're as radiant today as the sun on the waters. I trust you slept well? They're serving soup this morning, and some pheasant. Would you care for some wine?"

It was the custom of nobility to engage in such pointless enthusiasms; Desmos' show of partiality towards Sonja would have been quite in place on some lavish estate or townhouse. It was taken in that spirit by Desmos' peers. Sonja, however, took it for what it was; it was in her nature to discern the truth beneath the sham.

Gifted with this insight, which had sometimes saved her life and sometimes lent her wisdom, she did not regard Desmos' attentions as fawning or servile. Rather, she saw them as the aquired superficialities of a man who, thrown by fate into his duty, had done less with himself than he might have wished. Lord Sir Desmos, perhaps twice Sonja's age, had in his youth served as a warrior in the Aquilonian Guard; so much he had told Sonja. But certain favors from certain friends had gained him the entries necessary to rise, untempered, into court life. Given another time, another place, and Lord Sir Desmos might have been a man like her father a warrior, a farmer, a husband; a good man, honest with himself, strong and staunch; a gentle man until betrayed. Sonja sensed these virtues hidden in Sir Desmos although she did not greatly admire him; she had long since stopped searching for her father's spirit in any other man.

"Our ruffian seems to enjoy her fowl, judging from how she's wolfing it," said one highly-decorated woman to her thin husband—just loudly enough to be heard.

Sonja eyed her over the drumstick she had been munching on. "Aye, it's tasty, and even better for having been cooked in the open air, not smothered in some brick oven. If you can't finish yours, I'll be happy to do it for you."

The woman assumed a shocked air and looked away. Sonja suppressed a grin. Sir Desmos' thin moustaches curved slightly.

Sonja half-reached for the woman's pheasant and raised her eyebrows interrogatively, waiting. The woman, shocked still further at this brazen amazon's total lack of table etiquette, blanched and imploringly eyed the fat dowager to her left. Sir Desmos raised a nervous hand to his lips. Sonja shrugged, then took the piece of pheasant from the dowager's plate and dumped it on her own.

Wild laughter broke out among some of the low-lifes at the other end of the table.

Sonja widened her eyes in a show of innocence. Then, still playing her guileless role, she commented to a pasty-faced older man across from her, "Don't you find that ship voyages increase your appetite?"

He had not touched his plate; the color of his neck, which was fast rising to his cheeks, suggested that ship-voyages had exactly the opposite effect upon him.

"Don't they strengthen your appetite, Desmos?"

"Oh, to be sure, Sonja." She could see he was making an effort to avoid bursting out in laughter.

"Aye, there's nothing like a good voyage, with the rocking and waving of the ship, and the good clean air. It always makes me want to devour everything in sight, and top it off with sauces and jellies, and wash it down with good wine and ale, and—"

The unfortunate old man choked, gagged and lifted cupped hands to his mouth, then knocked his chair over in a sudden scramble to the rail.

The dowager whose pheasant Sonja had pilfered lost all control, sputtered, reached for her wine and grumbled under her breath about the class of persons certain Aquilonians were letting climb aboard ships these days.

Lord Sir Desmos sniggered, then blushed slightly and looked out to the passing shoreline. But the rough hewn traders at the lower end of the table let loose with reckless glee and wiped teary eyes.

Sonja, not a trace of a smile on her face, went on placidly chewing her breakfast and washing it down with wine.

"Tell me about yourself," said Sir Desmos. "Tell me who you are."

The sun was high but the day was becoming overcast, and a slight coolness began to be felt in the breeze. Sonja stood leaning on the starboard rail, staring down at the waters that lapped rhythmically against the *Niros'* hull.

"You know who I am."

"Yes, I know your name. But I want to know about your life. Who you are, what you are."

"Why?" Sonja did not face him, but she sensed his eyes on her.

"Because you intrigue me. You fascinate me. I like you."

Sonja smiled wryly. "You don't know me well enough to like or dislike me, Desmos. Maybe you like certain qualities in me."

"Certain qualities, then," he amended "—such as your wit; such as the insight you've just shown."

"Perhaps what truly intrigues you is that you don't know much about me."

Desmos laughed. "Perhaps. But I don't think I'll dislike you if I learn more."

Sonja glanced at him but did not reply.

"Why do you wear such armor?"

"Why do warriors wear armor?"

"Yours is hardly the sort most warriors wear. You say you come from Hyrkania. Were you born there?"

"Yes."

"How did you manage to become so deft with a sword?"

Sonja shifted her position on the rail. "How do you know I'm deft with a sword?"

"You must be, or you wouldn't wear it. Why saunter around asking for trouble unless you know you can handle yourself?"

She smiled slightly, caught the hint of devilishness in Lord Sir Desmos' eyes, and turned again to look at the far shore.

"You intrigue me, Red Sonja."

"You repeat yourself, Desmos."

"Have you ever been married?"

"Don't you think that's a little personal?"

"I'd like to know. I've been married three times."

"No. I've never married."

Desmos seemed to relax slightly.

"That makes you feel better for some reason?"

"I should have been extremely jealous."

More patrician patter—but now it made Sonja uncomfortable. "If you're thinking of asking me to become your wife, Desmos, the answer is no."

That seemed to strike him a real blow; he paled, and for an instant his face was a mixture of anger and chagrin. Then, trying to recapture his air of composure and light-heartedness, he said: "You mean that by no stretch of the imagination could you ever picture yourself as my wife?"

"Not yours, nor any man's."

"Surely you don't mean it!"

Sonja eyed him squarely. "I enjoy your company, Desmos. Don't spoil it, please."

"I don't mean to spoil it."

"Then you're succeeding handsomely despite your-self."

"Well, then, forgive me."

"Forgiven." Sonja grinned, and Desmos took it to heart. He touched her hand, patted it to re-secure their relationship—

She lifted her hand from the rail. "You're succeeding again."

Desmos sighed. He saw the dowager of breakfast time walking towards them, accompanied by one of her maidservants. Spotting Desmos and Sonja at the rail, she pivoted on her heel and headed back the way she had come, momentarily surprising the slave-girl who was trying to keep step with her mistress and fan her.

Desmos chuckled and nudged Sonja, who turned in time to see the old dowager making tracks away from them.

"Silly old bag," Sonja muttered, feeling some irrita-tion.

"That's the Lady Arure. She's—"

"—Not worth the energy it takes to call her names," Sonja stated decidedly. She turned to stare out across the waters. The broad, flat colors of the opposite bank of the Shirki looked cool and wild and inviting—part of the real world. Sonja glanced farther ahead, beyond the bow towards the far southern horizon, and spotted on the rim of the river a small splash of darker green-brown.

"An island?" she wondered aloud.

Desmos said nothing. Sonja turned, saw that his face had clouded with a frown.

"What island is that?" she asked.

Desmos voice was low as he answered: "It is the Isle."

"The Isle of what?"

"*Os Harku* is its full name, but it's usually just called 'the Isle'."

"I've never heard of it."

"It's a penal colony."

Sonja turned again at the tone of Desmos' voice and looked into his eyes. What did she see there? Pain? Guilt?

"A penal colony?"

"Aye. Some of the worst of Aquilonia's criminals are secured there—prisoners of war, traitors, violent offenders."

Sonja's brow creased.

"In my capacity as a director of court justice," Desmos continued, "I have probably sent at least a quarter of that island's population onto its shores."

"Does that trouble you?"

"Sometimes."

Sonja watched him.

"My life is a series of intense pressures, Sonja." Lord Sir Desmos' voice was a low monotone. "Perhaps that is why you—intrigue and delight me. Perhaps that's why I am so attracted to you. I can speak openly to you, for one thing—as I'm doing now—and you suspect no treachery, no hidden motive. The courts can be such an arena of hypocritical gaming! I have always been zealous in my regard for the law. Law is society; justice is what makes man not just another animal. I have ever felt thus, and it was due to my zeal—some might even say, my ruthlessness—in regard to the law that I managed to reach my present position of eminence."

Desmos paused.

"But—?" Sonja said, after a moment.

"But," he sighed, staring down at the washing waves, "—but, when my own brother committed a crime—a foul crime, a crime for which the law prescribed banishment to the Isle—for the first time in my life, I was torn. He committed murder in the cause of a political rebellion. He was young; his passions drove him to violent deeds against the throne he hated—and against the law—and I had to choose between blood or justice. I chose justice. I banished my younger brother to a life of hell amongst the human animals on that Isle."

Sonja was stunned. She could think of nothing to say.

"Since that day," Desmos went on after a pause, "I think I have become more lenient in my attitude. I know I have. Perhaps I thereby relieve some of the guilt I suffer for damning my brother to that colony. Perhaps that's why I so delight in slight moral infractions—why I love it when you bait these fat old women who wouldn't know how to urinate without a slave in attendance." He looked again to the Isle. "I've never visited there, never set foot on it—but the brother with whom I spent my happy childhood has been banished there for the rest of his days—and I put him there."

Sonja could think of no reply. She had sensed something in Lord Sir Desmos, and here it was—the personal devil which every man or woman carries sometime or other, sooner or later. The boulder hung around the neck that one presents to one's god when day is done and the night of the soul comes down.

Low thunder rumbled far away. Sonja looked to the sky. It darkened quickly. Faint flashes of heat lightning lit up the underside of the thick clouds above the opposite bank. Fat drops of rain began to spatter on the deck, in the waves, and against Sonja's face.

"It's time I went for some wine," Lord Desmos decided. He turned from Sonja, and went down the deck.

Sonja watched him as he retreated, while the falling rain whipped up quickly into sheets of cold mist, noisy on the boards of the deck.

The storm grew fierce. Strong winds drove the *Niros* on her perilous course. All passengers save a few had taken refuge in their cabins, where the wildness tossed them upon their berths and set many of the patrician women to pleading and praying and whining.

On deck, Tio eyed the angry skies, felt the enormous rocking of his ship and ordered his hands to furl sails and draw all lines tight. He cursed in Mitra's name and hung onto what was handy to save himself from being thrown to the deck. The man in the crow's nest cried out abjectly, fearful that he was being tossed over the side. Tio sent another sailor to relieve him, but he was so lashed by the wild winds that he could not make it up the shrouds.

Sonja was still on deck, hanging on to the ropes for safety and trying to make out anything distinct in the gray, swirling air. She could see nothing of the opposite shore. Occasional branches and twigs, torn from some section of land that Sonja guessed could not be too far away, clattered onto the *Niros'* decks or tangled in her lines.

Desmos was again on deck, beside Sonja. His manner was now sober, even grim.

"Can they tell where we're headed?" Sonja asked him, having to raise her voice so that Desmos, right beside her, could hear.

"No! It's impossible! But look ahead of us!"

Sonja turned. The wind and rains, formerly at her back, now pounded against her, almost taking her breath away. Just ahead, and off to starboard, she saw hints of shoreline—vague impressions lent by sudden pauses in the almost constant driving of wind and rain.

"Land!" she cried. "Teeth of Erlik! Has the storm driven us this close to the shore?"

Desmos gripped the rail, crouching against the buffeting. "Not the shore!" he yelled. "The Isle!"

Sonja's eyes went wide.

"If we strike land, it's the end!" Desmos yelled to her.

Behind them, high up on the poop, the pilot screamed in fear as his steering lines snapped. Sonja and Desmos turned to see Tio, swaying perilously, climb to aid the man. But instantly, with the snapping of the lines, the pilot's wheel revolved crazily. His right arm, caught between the spokes, broke; shrieking, the crippled pilot was dragged to the deck. Two men near him tried to fight the wheel and free his maimed arm while the pilot sobbed in agony, kicking his feet on the boards. Tio struggled up the ladders as lines snapped and timber cracked.

Sonja immediately made to run in and help, but Desmos grabbed her wet arm with a sure grip. Angrily she turned to face him.

"We can't help them!" Desmos cried. "They're gone! The whole steering-section's going!"

Sonja watched.

Tio was thrown back; he had to hold on to the slick timber to save himself from being thrown back down the way. The two men aiding the pilot had just managed to free his arm when they were picked up by an awesome swell and sent over the side. Sonja had a brief glimpse of their bodies, contorted and frozen in the gray blur of air, before they were swallowed by the mists. Then the pilot, shrieking in pain and trying to crawl in any direction for safety, was thrown down and sent skidding past Tio, who was holding on, down the stairs of the way. The man was dead as he landed on the waist-deck, his head broken, his blood diluting in the pouring rain.

Sonja broke from Desmos and ran to Tio; Desmos followed her. She knelt and helped the ship's master to his feet; dazed, Tio staggered and held on for support. He shook his head, wiped rain from his face. "The steering tackle's gone!" he moaned. "Now we'll hit that damned shore for certain!"

Desmos looked up and out over the starboard rail. The Isle was clear, now—fogged, blurred by the mists of wind and drenching rain, but clearly in their path. And the high thunder above their heads promised no soon end to the tempest.

Seamen were scurrying all over the decks, doing their best to lash down wayward lines and secure any broken timber. Loosed spars rattled this way and that over the decks. Men hanging for their lives onto the broken ratlines were lifted high into the air and swung out over the waves, then blown in over the decks again, their hands and boots tangled in the ropes, their faces pressed against the hard cord. More shrieks sounded intermittently as some sailors, losing their grip or caught unawares, were thrown over into the boiling, cold river or slammed haphazardly to the deck.

From below came some of the passengers—not the nobles, but the merchants and bankers and men of the street asking if they could help. Sailors slapped them on the back and called to them to do this or that task.

"Mitra—we're losing that mast! Haul down those ratlines! Tighten them!"

"Grab that line and secure it! Go on—two of you, get that line and—!"

"Help that man! Help him! Look out, she's rising—!"

Down below, damage was severe. Thrown furniture had struck heads and limbs, causing bruises and broken bones. The old dowager who had snubbed Sonja had left her cabin, fearing that it would be torn loose from the ship and sent skimming across the waves. Waddling up on deck, she screamed in terror at the sight of the wreckage and debris, the blood and corpses.

Tio yelled at her: "Arure!"

The dowager looked in all directions—then was suddenly struck by a vagrant spar and hurled to the deck. She slid across the slick boards and was dashed upon the gunwhale, falling plump and damp and lifeless.

Tio turned, saw a nearby line of trees, ghostly in the thick rain.

"The Isle!" he cried.

They were nearly upon it. The swollen river churned around them and the *Niros* was helpless in its hold. Sonja, Desmos and Tio watched, stunned impotent, as the damaged luxury ship raced down upon the rocks of the shoreline.

"Get down!" Tio cried to them. "Stay down! We'll be thrown over!"

Sonja was vividly aware of the deck beneath her feet: lurching, shoving, moving relentlessly with rhythmic risings and fallings towards those gray, overhanging trees, sharp shoreline rocks, tangled, huge roots that dipped into the river like gnarled veins sucking the life from the roaring water. Instinctively she pressed her boots to the deck, curling her toes, bunching her leg muscles, as if her tension could hold the ship back from her course.

The wind changed.

Sonja yelled. Great branches and limbs overhead scraped the masts and reefed sails of the *Niros*—

But the ship did not draw up onto the dangerous shore. Rather, she veered, slipped sidewise in the rolling waves and tacked—suddenly—twenty points to larboard.

Tio cursed in utter astonishment.

The wind seemed to be subsiding a bit. Sonja had a brief glimpse of what looked like a crowd bunched on the shoreline, vaguely hidden by blowing bushes and trees.

"Look—did you see them?" she called to Desmos.

"Dogs!" he howled. "Vultures! Scavengers! They're praying for us to be dashed to cinders—then they can steal aboard and loot. Even more, they'd like this ship so they can sail for freedom." He turned to Tio. "Break out oil—set fire to it!"

"What?"

"Take oil and tar and fire the ship!"

"Mitra's blood! Have you lost your—?"

"They'll take the ship! Don't you understand?" Desmos was screaming, frenzied, fearful. "They'll take the ship, otherwise! Didn't you see them? They're just waiting for us—they'll cut all our throats and take the ship!"

Sonja snarled at him, "Then we'll fight them!"

"Five hundred brigands?" Desmos seemed shocked at her stupidity.

"I won't fire my ship!" Tio roared, preparing to wrestle Desmos to the deck should the nobleman make any movement toward the stairs to below-decks.

A lurch—a rising swell. Desmos' reply was cut short

as he was forced to grab the starboard rail and hang on.
Tio looked up. A huge tree limb, hanging far out over
the river, had brushed against the *Niros'* mainmast.
Then Tio pointed.

Sonja saw, through the mist and falling rain, a man
with a knife in his hand, hanging high up on the limb. As
the *Niros* passed recklessly beneath him, he dropped.

Desmos moved back. Sonja drew her sword.

The man fell within the quarter deck, just missing the
way-steps leading to the poop. There was a crack as he
landed—an ankle or a leg breaking—but instantly in his
unheeding ferocity the exile was up, his knife out.
Though he was alone, there was a mad light in his eyes
as if he believed himself accompanied by a thousand
avenging demons.

Screaming insanely, he lifted high his blade and ran
limping towards them.

Sonja's sword was up. She jumped ahead, and as the
hate-frenzied rogue whirled his knife crazily and randomly around him, stepped in with a graceful lunge and
skewered him through the chest.

The man reeled back, yet incredibly found the
strength to step ahead a few paces. Sonja tensed for a
second thrust—but then the dog pitched headlong to the
boards, slamming down on his face, his knife skittering
away, his head jumping nervously and his hands clawing
as death took hold.

Low thunder rumbled, sounding far away. Sonja,
staring at the corpse as the rain washed his blood from
her steel, noticed that the tremendous wind had quiet-
ened quickly.

Too quickly.

She turned to Tio and Desmos.

"There'll be more," Tio yelled. "Get swords—all of
you. Hurry!" He turned to Sols, his first mate, and
threw him a key. "Take down the weapons. Every man
is to have a sword and dirk. Do it!"

Sols caught the key and hurried below deck.

The rain still came down; the river yet rocked the galley from side to side. But the *Niros* made its way almost placidly, hugging the shore of the Isle, weaving beneath the tree limbs and away from rocks and roots as if guided by some giant invisible hand.

A few sailors had run off with Sols to get the weapons. Many others, plus those passengers who had come up from below, were collected in the waist and beside the forecastle, watching Tio, waiting for his orders.

And Tio, wondering at the *Niros'* strange conduct, stared at the shore line. "Two of you men," he called, not looking behind, "—get over the poop and check that tackle."

No one moved.

"Now!" He turned, wrathful, and his gaze happened upon two men. "You and you—get over the rail!"

They went—slowly at first, then quickly—up the way.

As they reached the pilot wheel, one of the men screamed and fell back with an arrow through his chest.

All faces turned to him. The second man dropped to his knees and frantically crawled down the stairs, back to his fellows.

Still the barge crawled, ever more slowly, along the shoreline.

"It's the Isle of the Damned!" breathed a sailor.

A sudden quiet gripped them, a vague feeling of magic or fate in the air. The unreality of it—buffeted by the worst storm any of them had ever lived through, then experiencing the uncannily abrupt end of that storm, and now being *guided* up against the shore of Os Har-ku. . .

The eyes of all on deck peered quietly from damp, sweaty, strained faces into the dark foliage of the Isle—watching for any hint of movement, for the flash of weapons, for a tribe of the Damned to suddenly burst upon them and attack . . .

Sonja glanced at Desmos, then at Tio, whose stare was constantly upon the rank foliage of the Isle.

The *Niros*, crawling now so slowly that it seemed scarcely to move at all, scraped drily upon roots and limbs. Desmos swallowed, fingering the jeweled court-dagger at his waist.

Sonja whispered to Tio, "We've got to try repairing the tackle again. I'll go up."

Desmos looked at her. Tio shook his head.

A clatter came from behind them—Sols, calling for men to help him with the weapons.

Behind him and the other sailors, groups of patricians began to show their faces.

"Hurry!" Tio urged in a low voice. "A sword and dirk for each man!"

Desmos took a sword. Sonja tightened her grip on hers.

Then, as a ray of warm sunlight broke through the high gray clouds, the silently-moving barge struck a sand bar and skidded, rolled, but made still.

Chapter 3

"Sizzle me in Hell!" swore Urdus. "It's a ship!"

"As Athu predicted!" Aleil exclaimed. "Exactly as Athu said it would be!"

Urdus glared uneasily, shook his head, snorted.

They were on a trail, walking through the rich, damp forest, on their way to the shoreline. One of Urdus' rogues had come running up to the caves to report that, in the midst of the storm, an Aquilonian barge had made port on the beach as neatly and cleanly as if she had dropped anchor on the stillest of days. Already inmates were massing there, lusting to take her . . .

Now, crouched behind covering foliage, Urdus and Aleil and dozens of convicts stared in wonder at the sorcerous miracle of a ship ready and waiting for them, just beyond this fringe of trees.

"Gods of the Hells!" Urdus exclaimed. "It's a fatship!" Such did pirates and looters call any vessel that sported more silk than cord, that housed more idle vacationers than honest sea-faring men.

"We'll have no trouble gutting her," muttered a man behind him, thumbing his knife-blade.

"Call the wizard," Urdus commanded. He faced one of his men. "You—get going! Find him!"

"But he's in the southwestern swamps," the rogue protested.

"You have legs—use them before I break them!"

The man turned and strode rapidly back up the trail.

"It may be dangerous," said Aleil. "The Isle's aroused, now. Everyone will want a piece of this rich prize."

Urdus growled maliciously. "That's why I want that damned Shemite. Nobody else will get this ship. He promised it to me!"

The Shemite, however, was not far off. Urdus' messenger had taken only a dozen steps back down the trail when he came up face to face with him.

"Urdus wants you," the man told Athu.

"I know." The wizard passed by him as silently as if he were a wind, as noiselessly as if he floated just above the carpet of the earth. In the shadowed forest his eyes seemed to glow with an eerie light.

Water droplets sprayed from the leaves and brambles as Athu broke through the foliage and came up behind Urdus. The giant Vanir turned to face him.

"You've done me right, Athu. Damn me, but your words were true!" His tone somehow suggested contempt mixed with praise, thanks with arrogance.

Athu said nothing.

Aleil watched the wizard. "Everyone else on the Isle will come running for this prize," she told him. "You must help us steal the ship and hold it!"

Still Athu said nothing.

Aleil was puzzled. "What's the matter with you, Shemite?"

He suddenly cast upon her eyes full of anger and wrath, and in a voice so low that it moved not even the wet, heavy air he whispered, "My work is my own."

"What?" Aleil asked him, puzzled. She experienced an uncomfortable atmosphere from the sorcerer; the sense of his sorcerous will, his power.

Urdus was less concerned. "Will you help us take that ship?" His voice was strong.

Athu glanced at him.

"Will you?" Urdus repeated more loudly. "Others

will be coming soon. Word spreads quickly on the Isle. We must attack now!" He waited impatiently for Athu's response.

The Shemite stood as he was, sinister, self-absorbed. Urdus' men became uncomfortable. The wizard was staring through the trees, watching the quiet Aquilonian barge as if by force of concentration he might set it afire, or lift it into the air, or send it back upon its old course by conjuring another storm.

Urdus' sweaty hand tightened on his sword.

"Fool," Athu said at last. "I'll help you take the ship, but you must promise me one thing in return."

"What is it?" Urdus snarled, wary of a trap.

"The life's blood of all who die aboard her."

Urdus was stunned; then he felt an urge to bawl out with huge laughter. But Athu's face showed no trace of humor.

"There'll be life's blood aplenty," Urdus growled. "More than you can use for your sorcery, wizard. Take it!" Urdus growled. "Take it all, and welcome!" Then he motioned his men ahead. "Arrows first," he ordered, quietening his tone. "Fire when I give the word. Then we board her. Quietly, now—and some of you bowmen, up into the trees. Stay behind the foliage till I tell you to move!"

Sonja stood at the starboard rail, flanked by Master Tio and Lord Desmos and sundry sailors, all armed. Behind them were gathered the many nobles and merchants, protecting their wives and women—all on deck, waiting. The air was still.

Sonja tensely regarded the dark forest, her blue eyes fixed with the stare of a predatory beast. Behind her, she heard the hushed murmurs and whimperings of a number of the patrician women. Despite the deaths so far, despite the storm and the imminent peril, some of them even confessed a thrill at the excitement they were going through.

Red Sonja silently cursed them.

She ignored Desmos, who out of his tenseness had just made some urbane comment—then the first of the arrows struck.

They came from everywhere—a hail of shafts flying from the foliage, raining down from the heights of the trees overhead, showering the starboard side of the *Niros.*

"Duck!" yelled Sonja. "All of you!"

Screams answered her yell. She heard splashes as sailors dropped from the lines or toppled over the sides into the water. The nobles and merchants behind, all armed, drew back and threw their arms out to hold back their women. Tio yelled commands to maintain order.

Sonja, crouching, drew herself up cautiously to peer over the rim of the rail. "Tarim!" she cursed.

A horde of brigands were splashing into the water along the shoreline, led by a huge man who roared orders to them and waved a sword as long as some of his warriors.

"Fall back!" Sonja yelled. "Don't scatter—form a group!"

A number of attackers had dropped into the *Niros'* lines from above; Sonja glanced up, saw how they were climbing out on the huge limbs of overhanging trees and thence clambering to the decks. Tio's sailors were trying to meet their charge. The blades of swords and knives began to clatter together.

"Fall back, in Erlik's name!" Sonja howled. "Group!"

She jumped away from the rail, backing into the waist, sensing that that first volley of arrows had been a tactic to stun the ship's crew into disorganization, allowing the attackers to board. Tio sensed the same thing.

"Back!" he roared to his men. "Stand back—await the charge. Then rush in and split their heads as they climb above the rail!"

When the ruffians appeared, swords met them.

Hands, lifting over the side for purchase, were lopped off; faces thrusting into view were hewn asunder with bloody strokes. Sonja was there with the first to move against the attack; as a bearded rogue hauled himself up onto the rail, sword out, she leapt at him, slicing his arm. The pirate lost his balance and Sonja's sword, piercing his throat, finished him. He toppled back over the rail, dragging two of his comrades into the water with him.

But the numbers of the attackers were too great. Sonja and Tio and the sailors could not manage to hold them back at the rail. The islanders continued to drop from the shrouds, and some of them had taken the chance of swimming out to board the *Niros* from bow and poop and larboard.

Yet several of them met death in that way, for the instant blood had appeared in the water, so had the crocodiles and fat, carnivorous serpents that roamed the shoreline. They slid greasily into the water to feast, and in moments attackers were being pulled under, shrieking and threshing.

Sonja, beating back another of Urdus' warriors, sent the man screaming over the side with blood trailing from his belly, saw him fall into the open jaws of a huge crocodile. The rogue shrieked wailingly, uselessly waving his sword as the great white-toothed jaws clamped surely about his middle and dragged him, foaming, under the gray waters.

But now Urdus' men were on board the *Niros* in greater numbers than Tio's crew could manage. The men of the Aquilonian barge were sailors, seasoned men who knew ships and the sea and life—but they were not trained swordsmen nor veteran warriors. Most of Urdus' men had been killers; they were hardened to lives of crime and handy with the sword. They had lived in violence and recklessness; they understood better than Tio's sailors, and certainly better than the nobles and merchants, how life can hang by the thinnest of threads

—how it often demands split-second awareness, instant reaction, unsubtle defense.

Sonja, too, understood this—consciously and instinctively. At every hint or premonition of danger her guard was expertly up, and in the space of a heartbeat her sword had flashed out and done its work.

Tio—stout, slow, but once a man of weapons—showed a rough-and-ready skill at deployment; it encouraged Sonja to see how easily and intuitively he ordered his men to take this position, secure the foredeck, buttress the flanks . . .

But his men were not soldiers—and the merchants and nobles, who had seldom had to face life squarely, certainly did not know how to face death.

Desmos among them.

Sonja, battling for her life against the swarming wave of criminals, handled herself expertly as the battle surged around her, as the screams filled the air and the clack of swords rose in a deafening clamor, as the blood spurted madly upon deck and mast and canvas. Nostrils flared, blue eyes sparkling furiously, crimson hair flowing, she charged and killed and charged again. The criminals, amazed to see this woman dressed in scant armor and managing a sword so handily, almost seemed to fight one another for a chance to meet her—

And go down at her sword's point.

The crowded decks became slick with blood. Sonja nearly tripped several times over the corpses that were piling up. She cut one furiously charging rogue across the face, twisted just in time to avoid the razor edge of a blade missing the small of her back so closely that she felt the coolness of fanned air. Lithely she turned, saw the sword raised again, and deftly—with the split-second grace and calm and certainty that comes to those skilled in any art—she feinted sidewise and lunged. The cur, skewered, dropped his sword and clattered to the deck.

She heard Tio howl in exultation at making another

kill. And then she saw Desmos. The nobleman was cowering—shrunken into a corner against the bulkhead of the forecastle—cringing, alone and half-hidden as the swirl of battle raged about him.

Sonja, stunned, jumped towards him.

"Fight!" she yelled.

Desmos had his sword held out before him, the weakest of defenses, as if hoping that any possible attacker might blunder into its point.

"Fight, Desmos!"

In a voice that rattled with shame, "I—I cannot fight . . ."

"Take your sword and—!"

"I cannot *fight!*" he rasped loudly, staring at Sonja with eyes full of horror—staring, not at her face, but at the bloody point of her sword which wavered so threateningly before her.

Grunts and yells sounded behind her. Sonja crouched and spun as a silvery arc flashed above her, just where her head had been. She lunged, caught her attacker squarely through the chest, and left him reeling on his feet as she whirled to meet the thrust of a second assailant. She jumped, side-stepped, was about to parry with expert skill—when something pulled her from behind and she was thrown off balance.

Curled claws, the fingers of the man she had just skewered, gripped her hair, scraped her naked back and caught the clasp of her scale-mail halter. The dog, dying, was seeking to haul her down.

Sonja tried to evade the lunge of the ruffian before her, had to make do with a fouled sweep which totally missed the man's face. The brute barked a laugh, leaped forward. Sonja felt her knees buckling as the dying man, still clutching her with a death-grip, fell to the decks.

"Desmos!" she yelled. "Help!"

But she was pulled back. Only the faulty timing of her assailant allowed her to stave off his stroke and plunge her blade through his bowels. He staggered away, screaming, as blood spilled thickly from his ripped leather tunic.

And still Sonja was pulled back. She struggled desperately and her mail halter, its clasp bursting from the strain, dropped free and clattered to the boards. The air was suddenly cool on her freed breasts.

But still the dying maniac kept a relentless hold on her. Sonja kicked and fell on her side, frantic in the fear that any sword might now cut her open or behead her.

The brigand's face was gray as that of a lich; his hands, curled into claws, tore down Sonja's back and hips in furrows that drew blood as she struggled. In his death throes, he sought to bite her calf; Sonja pulled back and kicked him in the teeth. Unheeding, he groped for the knife that she wore strapped to her thigh. Agonized, feeling more and more vulnerable as the precarious instants passed, Sonja jammed one elbow into the deck and lunged desperately ahead.

The rogue screamed, missing the knife—but as Sonja squirmed away he took her mail-skirt with him, even as his hands froze and his breath rattled to final silence.

A knife thudded into the wood by Sonja's head, clamping a lock of her scarlet hair to the deck as she lifted up. She struggled ahead again, digging her elbows against the wood; the taloned claws trailed down her legs and fell free. Her elbows, battered, sent shards of pain up her arms and into her wrists, but she still gripped her sword.

A bloody boot thudded near her and Sonja rolled over, up into a crouch. As the attacker's sword swept at her again she leapt forward, blade straight out before her. She had a fleeting impression of a glowering, bearded face before it exploded in a bath of scarlet.

Sonja whirled and half crouched. Naked but for her sword-belt, knives and Nemedian boots, she looked like some primitive goddess of war, some legendary queen of slaughter brandishing her red-stained blade.

In an instant she was back into the battle. Screaming

faces whirled about her. She saw Tio with a group of his
sailors, holding his own on the bow, slashing away at
any who came to oppose him. But it was useless, Sonja
realized—there were too many Aquilonian corpses, too
many sailors and merchants and nobles lying with
throats slit, faces hacked, bowels pushing from slashed
stomachs. Severed legs and arms, gore-trailing, twitched
on the decks with the final signs of fleeing life.

She made for Tio, downed two renegades who were
hacking at him, and jumped up on the bow-deck to his
side. Now their swords clattered in unison as they
fought side by side, and through the wheeling flashes of
silver and crimson Sonja caught glimpses of Urdus—a
giant dressed in leather and black fur, handling his great
sword as if born with it, killing sailor after sailor.

She heard the screams of the women, saw one of them
captured by five of the criminals and thrown to the deck.
She was not a young woman, but these men were more
angry than lustful. They tore her flimsy clothes from her
and threw her on her back, slapped her, tore her legs
apart. Screams shrilled.

Someone came at Sonja and she spun, snarling. She
never saw his face, only a hint of his sword and a hairy,
veined arm as she parried and ploughed her sword low
into his guts, heard him shriek, saw him fall backwards
split from naval to groin, blood spurting in a thick trail.

"The boats!" Tio grated, his voice harsh from exertion.

"We can't—!" A thrust, a howl, and another foe's
blood leapt into Sonja's face, ran down her cheek.

"We must! They're backing off. Break for it—cut
loose a dinghy and jump for it!"

Sonja gasped. No swords lunged for her. Momentarily she absorbed the scene of slaughter. Three convicts
had a screaming merchant bent back over the rail; blood
spurted and runneled as their knives cut long, crazy lines
from his chest to his groin.

"They'll be at us again in a moment," Tio growled.

"The big one's after them to quit looting and get back to fighting. Hurry up with that dinghy, damn it!"

"Desmos is in the waist!" Sonja cried suddenly.

"Leave him!"

Tio ran. Sonja watched him, undecided. Behind her loud yells sounded, and a thrown knife fanned her flesh as it narrowly missed her. Sonja cursed. Yet, still no rush came. Many of the rogues were already looting below decks.

Some of Tio's men had cut loose a life boat, dropped it into the water and jumped after it. The criminals watching them seemed undecided whether to attack or avoid further risk and let the survivors go.

Tio severed the lines of another dinghy. "Come, Sonja —hurry!"

Sonja looked behind her, sword ready. She saw a man running in her direction from the shadow of the gangway, his face bloody, being chased by another man waving a sword.

"Desmos!"

He screamed when he saw her. The brute behind him hove up his sword even as Desmos reached for the low rail separating the decks. Sonja darted forward and the pursuer stumbled, skewered through the eye by her nimble blade.

"Run, Desmos!"

"Come on!" Tio yelled as his dinghy splashed into the water.

Sonja snarled as she saw that up both ways to the forecastle new lines of attackers were hurrying, leaping over fallen bodies. She grabbed Desmos by his shirt and pants, heaved him up and hauled him over the side. He dropped, yelling and threshing, straight into the water.

Sonja followed—her boots clearing the rail just as a sword split the wood.

The murky water dimmed her hearing as she splashed into it and swirled about, kicking, striking out with her free hand and holding onto her sword with the other.

When she surfaced, gasping, feeling the bite of the water in her many wounds, she cast about for the small boat. It was only a spear's-length distant.

"Hurry!" Tio cried.

Sonja saw Desmos swimming behind her, both hands free. He had dropped his sword.

Above, criminals cursed. A knife or two were thrown —but Tio's men were bending their backs at the oars, and the dinghies were starting away from the barge. The rogues on the ship were mostly laughing, pointing, making no serious effort to slay the fleeing survivors.

Sonja dog-paddled as best she could; Tio held out his hand to her and pulled her aboard. The he yelled to Desmos, "Kick water, damn your patrician hide!"

"Tarim!" Sonja yelled, pointing.

White-toothed jaws rose out of the water behind Desmos who, not noticing, thought his greatest danger lay in not making the escaping boat.

"Swim, Desmos! Damn you, swim!"

He threw out a hand. Sonja grabbed for it. The open jaws neared. Desmos missed; he kicked his legs, threw out his hand again.

Sonja reached.

The criminals on the *Niros* howled in glee.

Desmos cast a look behind him—then screamed and kicked frantically.

Sonja stood upright, drew one of her thigh-knives and hurled it, skewering the crocodile's white maw. Blood spurted from the thick tongue; the jaws clamped shut as if on prey and the thing dove, its huge tail splashing the thick water.

Tio held out his hand to Desmos, who grabbed it and nearly pulled the portly captain into the river in his struggle to get aboard. Clambering over the side, he dropped prone in the bow, whimpering.

Tio looked at Sonja—and then his expression changed.

"You're naked!" he cried, noticing it for the first time.

"I know." Sonja looked past him, to the receding *Niros*. Then she whispered: "What the hell?"

Tio followed her gaze. "More?" he wondered aloud.

They could clearly see figures on the deck; the criminals who had taken the ship—and among them, a man dressed in a dark robe of animal skins.

Then came sounds of renewed battle from the *Niros*.

"Are they fighting among themselves?" Sonja asked.

Tio shook his head. "Look," he rasped "in the trees, on the shore—more of them from the island, fighting to take control!"

Sonja cursed and threw up an arm, pointing. "Tarim! Look at them!"

They could see it clearly now: the bloody criminals, whom they had fought, engaged in duels with other convicts—and then the man in animal skins, raising his fists to the heavens, screamed in a language none of them had ever heard.

"Laikada-ayalz, kalhun, na Arkatu—"

Distant thunder knelled.

"Sorcery!" Sonja breathed.

They heard frantic screams aboard the ship as a miasmic haze, like hot air above a fire, formed slowly out of the air about the *Niros*. And as Tio and Sonja and the pausing rowers of the dinghy watched, numberless men shrieked in agony and jumped—or were somehow hurled—from the decks of the ship.

They seemed to be on fire. Yet the ship was not aflame; the sorcerer in his animal skin cloak stood holding his fists in the air, unmoving, while his howling victims were pulled up in crowds and tossed overboard by some supernatural agency. Into the waters of the River Shirki they splashed, where they still burned as they sank—where the water did not douse the flames . . .

"Row!" Tio yelled, both anger and fear in his voice. "Row, damn you! There's an Aquilonian guardhouse a league upriver." Still he stared at the *Niros*.

Sonja glanced behind, to the other row boat. Only the two had escaped.

"That's all of us, then," she said. Tio did not answer. He watched the *Niros* a bit longer, then dropped his gaze to Desmos, finally looked at Sonja.

"You're a fine figure of a woman," he said matter-of-factly.

Sonja rubbed her bruised and scratched legs, wiped blood from her arms and breasts. She shrugged.

"Here—" Tio removed his coarse seaman's shirt and handed it to Sonja. Instead of putting it on, she drew it around her waist and tied the long sleeves over one hip, making of it a skirt.

"Can you spare me your belt?"

Tio nodded. "I guess my belly'll hold up by breeches. I'd offer you them, too, but I have to protect my own . . . you understand." He unfastened his belt and gave it to her.

Tio looked back at the *Niros*. "All of them—dead . . ." There was an emptiness in his tone.

Sonja's gaze dropped to Desmos, who had propped himself in the bow of the dinghy and was still gasping for air. He did not look at her.

Again she looked to the *Niros*. It was silent now, and the rowers had made far from it, but for the moment Sonja thought of only one thing—not the slaughter, nor Tio nor Desmos.

Sorcery.

It explained what had happened, explained the strange fear in the air.

Sorcery . . .

Aboard the *Niros,* Urdus strode slowly and proudly upon the bloodstained decks, his great sword in one hand, boots caked with cruor, beard matted thickly with drying blood. All about him worked his victorious desperados—three score of them, women as well as men—cleaning the boards, repairing rope and tackle and split canvas.

Urdus looked to the poop, where a crowd of men

were standing at the rail, feeding over line and watching down the ship's side.

"Is the steering fixed?" he bawled out.

"Nearly," called one of the men.

Urdus smiled with satisfaction. He looked out at the broad gray Shirki, and saw no sign of the few survivors who had fled the barge. He looked towards the island, and imagined there crowds of prisoners, penal colonists eager to attempt another battle yet fearful of the slaughter which had befallen their comrades at Athu's hands.

Athu . . .

Urdus' men were dumping the slain over the rails and in answer to the splashes of the gashed corpses came the predators of the shoreline—the crocodiles and serpents, feasting as they had never feasted before, upon the banquet of human flesh.

And up from the cabins of the *Niros* came looters with the spoils—gems, bracelets and jeweled ceintures, coffers full of gold and silver—the amassed wealth of those merchants and businessmen who had been aboard. The pirates cackled and jested riotously as they celebrated their taking of such piled riches.

Also from the ship's interior emerged the Shemite. He held in his hands one plain box, made of cedar fastened with copper and bronze. It was rather large and lined with silk, but contained no wealth.

Athu, however, had not taken this box for its value.

Attaining the mid-deck, he prowled silently for a moment, then drew up sharply as he realized that Urdus' men were casting overboard the many corpses which the battle had reaped. He approached Urdus angrily.

"What are you doing?"

Urdus eyed the stocky Shemite warily. "I'm cleaning up the boat."

"You are throwing away my corpses!"

Aleil, nearby, edged closer towards Urdus, watching Athu. Others close by dropped what they were doing, letting go of corpse or main-cord, to stare nervously at the wizard, whom they had come to fear.

Urdus remembered what he had promised the Shemite. "They'll begin to stink, Athu. You know as well as I that the litter of war is the breeding ground of unclean death."

Athu stared at him venomously.

Urdus never averted his gaze, but his face paled a bit in the warm sunshine. In a lowered voice, he said: "Use those corpses which remain."

Athu growled, "I was promised all of them."

"A god's lot remains!" countered Urdus, sword shivering with anger in his tensing fist. "Take them!"

"I shall need a god's lot and more," Athu answered grimly. A "god's lot" was a common Aquilonian expression; drawn from religious parable, it added to three-score and thirteen.

Then, ignoring the frightened stares of the warriors about him and the hatred that glared from Urdus' eyes, Athu turned to those corpses nearest him on the mid-deck, muttered something unintelligible even to those who stood closest to him, and raised one fist in the air while holding his cedar box in the other.

Instantly the blood of the slain corpses, rich within torn wounds and flowing wetly upon the scarred deck boards, pulled into the air and misted into a scarlet gas, then collected like a whirling funnel into the Shemite's box. Gasps arose from the crowd of criminals, and they drew back.

"What is he *doing?*" Aleil gasped, clutching Urdus' heavy chest from behind.

From corpse to corpse, pile to pile, Athu sauntered. He muttered to himself and raised his fist into the air, and in answer the blood that lay at his feet, from one corpse or many, funneled up in lines of scarlet smoke and, gathering like a plume of red incense following a will of its own, dipped down into the box.

No one looked into that box to see how the mists collected, nor did any wish to approach that near to Athu.

Athu's grisly chore took little more than half an hour. The sun sank lower, gaining a ruddy tinge of late afternoon as Athu made his silent way from mid-deck to poop, down the port side towards the foredeck, then back again to the starboard side of the mid-deck where he had begun. Not one of the criminals had moved from his or her position as the Shemite made his circuit.

Then, done, Athu closed his cedar-wood box. Not a whisp or a breath of scarlet fume escaped it as the lid fell shut; nor did the sorcerer bother to lock it, merely snapping the copper hasp on the front of it into place. Without deigning to notice Urdus or any of the others on deck, Athu made his way down into the hold to take his rest.

He had taken Captain Tio's cabin for his own. Nobody objected.

As if breaking a spell, Urdus bawled, "On with it! Get rid of those corpses! Fasten those lines!" Galvanized, his followers took up where they had left off.

But now there were no blood stains on the decks, nor did blood drip upon the planks as the bodies were discarded—nor did it film the waters of the Shirki to attract predators.

"Is that steering tackle fixed?" Urdus yelled to the men on the poop.

"Aye, Urdus! She's ready to sail!"

"And those sails?"

"Aye, Urdus!" came responding voices.

"Then set her under! We're free!"

Cheers answered him, and men took various stations to unfurl canvas and tighten lines. Three fought for the pilot's place until Urdus himself took command and spun the spoked wheel to free it from the tangled brush, while gusts of wind bellied the great Aquilonian sails and pushed the groaning *Niros* out into the mainstream.

Aleil, keeping near to Urdus, reclined against the poop rail but found her gaze straying to the way steps which Athu had taken to the hold.

"What about him?" Urdus asked suddenly, turning about to face her.

Aleil shrugged, but her eyes flashed. Her great wave of black hair fanned about her tanned face, and she smiled amiably at Urdus, shrugging again, as if to say that she was too overjoyed at their escape from the island to care about the Shemite.

But Urdus was in a foul mood. He grunted deeply, turned away from her, and steered the *Niros*.

And Aleil's smile faded as she stared at the steps leading to below-decks.

A few impotent arrows, angrily launched, whistled through the air far behind them and sliced into the waters of the Shirki—the disconsolate reprisals of those left on the Isle, left behind while Urdus in his galley, with his crew and his Shemite sorcerer made his way away, free and unhampered.

Veljo, watching from the brush, waved away mosquitoes and shook this head, then turned away from the shore to begin his search for his supper.

Chapter 4

"Now you look more like a warrior," Tio told Sonja, "and less like a woman playing games with warrior's garb."

Sonja smirked. "Is that what you thought of me?"

"Frankly," he confided, reaching to replenish his wine, "when I first saw you, I wondered if you were some nobleman's harem girl." He smiled and shook his head.

Sonja smirked again, then moved this way and that on her toes, testing out her new mail tunic. "A trifle snug at the hips," she complained, "and the skirt's too long— can't have my legs chafed because of rusty Aquilonian link mail."

"That armor'll never rust," Tio promised her, taking pride in the workmanship of his compatriots. "And Aquilonian men usually wear breeches when they put on those glories."

"Allow me some freedom of movement, will you? It's bad enough I've added ten pounds already. The sleeves have got to go, at least."

"You're a woman at heart, Sonja," Tio observed. "Can't leave well enough alone."

"I could take offense at that."

"Did it ever occur to you that these things are designed for battle?"

"Tio, old man, what my previous armor lacked in

modesty it more than made up for in allowing me un-hampered movement. Look you!" With a flourish Sonja whipped free her blade and lunged towards the window-sill.

"Still quick as an eel."

"I feel slower than rising bread."

"You just pinioned some rascal's belly to the window ledge!"

"I just gave him ample time to lop my head from my shoulders." Wrathfully Sonja removed the link mail tunic and, ignoring Tio's ogling, proceded to use her knife in sawing the cords that held sleeve to shoulder.

"Have you no shame?" Tio asked.

"Shame is in the mind of the beholder, my friend." One heavy sleeve fell to the floor and Sonja kicked it away; then she worked to free the other.

"Would that my wife—my ex-wife—had been so en-dowed by Ishtar! I'd never have gone to sea."

"What a lecher. She probably kicked you out of her house, and that's why you went a-sailing. There!" The other sleeve dropped free. Sonja pulled the tunic on once more, nodding with pursed lips at the freedom the sleevelessness allowed her.

She sat down opposite Tio and pushed a goblet across the small table between them. He poured for her.

"Seriously," he said, "that mail-shirt really is a great improvement over your previous armor—or lack of it, rather. Tell me, whatever possessed you to design such an impractical outfit?"

"I didn't design it. You weren't far wrong, Tio, com-paring it to some harem girl's garb. It was designed for me with something like that in mind—not by a nobleman, but by a regent of Hyrkania."

Tio leaned forward, intrigued.

"His army captured the mercenary band I was with," Sonja went on, "and his soldiers brought me to his pal-ace in Khorlu. The fat swine had me paraded before him like a slave-whore at auction, then announced that he found me to his liking and that I would be one of his concubines. He seemed amused when I protested that I was a soldier, and had his metal workers design that mockery of armor for me.

"The whole story is too involved to go into now. I'll say only that I managed to slay the pig when he tried to possess me, then escaped from his palace and from Hyrkania. Since then I've often worn that costume, even in battle—just for the pleasure of disemboweling any man who chose to make an issue of it."

Tio whistled. He could barely sense a restrained fury behind the woman's even, matter-of-fact tone.

"You're one of a kind, Sonja—and, by Mitra, if *I've* ever offended you, I hasten to apologize!"

Sonja laughed. "You're not sword-bait, Tio, and you know it."

"Thank Mitra! But isn't it a risky luxury, provoking dangerous men?"

"Aye. Perhaps I'll give it up. Still, it was worth it to me. I've proven myself a better fighter than any of the men who mocked me. After all, I'm alive. They're all dead. And I've never regretted killing a single one of them."

Tio looked away, deciding to change the subject. He noticed the dimming of daylight at the window.

"Sundown," he said sadly. "I hope those officers have made up their minds by now."

"Have you seen Desmos?" Sonja asked him.

Tio scowled. "He was with them. He'd better not be spinning any yarns about his heroism against those pirates."

"Leave him alone. I doubt that he's—"

"I'd think you'd be the first to condemn him."

"A man can't help what he is. If Desmos has to live with the fact that he's sword shy, then it's bad enough without our pecking at him about it."

"Suppose your life depended on him lifting his sword."

"It didn't come to that."

"Not quite." Tio belched, took another swig of wine.

"But a man has no right to carry a blade unless he can use it."

"He claimed that he did use it, and well, in his younger days."

"I can't say. But it only serves to warn me again that people are never what they appear."

"I learned that lesson long ago."

"No doubt." Tio twirled his goblet, then gulped more wine. "But I'd trust a rogue before I'd trust a nobleman. At least you have a better guess as to where you stand. If a rascal turns out good, you're pleasantly surprised; but if a nobleman turns out to be a fool, and you've staked yourself on him—"

The door opened. An Aquilonian soldier stepped in and saluted. "Commander Hubarthis invites you to supper now."

"Damned well about time," Tio grumbled, rising and steadying himself with one hand upon the table.

"Need help?" Sonja said, smiling, gesturing towards the door.

"I've drunk more than fishes," Tio answered her scornfully, "and I could drink you from here to the next full moon. 'Need help . . . .' Bah!"

"I've drunk with the best of them," Sonja countered lightly.

"Oh? And how well did you do?"

She smiled at the Aquilonian but made no answer, then followed him out the door. *Men are seldom what they seem*, she thought. *You bluster, Tio, but you'd cry like a lost child over that ship and those passengers, if we left you alone with your wine.*

They were led across the compound of the Aquilonian fort, into the main building that housed the government offices. Here Sonja and Tio found Commander Hubarthis and his staff, seated at a long table. The company rose to bid them welcome.

"Please be seated," said Hubarthis, gesturing politely.

Sonja and Tio took chairs; Sonja eyed Lord Desmos, but he averted his gaze, ashamed.

Hubarthis was a tall, well built, handsome man sporting a moustache and a neatly trimmed beard. It seemed that soldiers stationed on the frontiers could get away with such innocent excesses. He gave the impression of being a proud, determined and very capable man, and seemed chagrined at this recent turn of events.

"Please," Hubarthis indicated the wine at hand. "Help yourselves. Captain Tio, your men are being fed now in the barracks. The stewards will bring out our plates in a moment."

Tio helped himself to another goblet of wine, eyeing Sonja to make sure that she saw him. Sonja noticed, but did without wine for herself.

"I think you should know," Hubarthis began, "that this is a very serious matter, and one which I'm not taking lightly. I've readied a ship, and as soon as supper is done we'll set sail after the *Niros*. I've already dispatched a boat full of troops under the command of Major Thobis to canvas the eastern shore, and I've sent word both north and south for other garrisons to be on the lookout. We'll find your ship, Captain Tio."

Tio nodded.

"I've also sent a messenger to the capital," Hubarthis continued. "We've taken down the names of those who survived in your two dinghies—so this list will be compared to the embarkation records in Tarantia."

"That may take time," Tio told him. "We didn't set sail from the capital, and they forward those logs only once a month."

"In which case," Hubarthis told him in turn, not pausing at all, "official action will be taken. They know how to deal with such matters. Close family members will probably be told that the deaths occurred in a storm; the true nature of this affair will likely be kept confidential. It's better to avert a panic, and a rebellion on the Isle will certainly cause enough official headaches. Which is why I want to settle the matter as quickly as possible."

"I'll want to sail with you," Tio reminded him.

"Of course."

"And I," Sonja interjected. "I'm a soldier, and my sword's for hire."

Commander Hubarthis gravely arched an eyebrow, but answered diplomatically, "Well, we'll see . . ."

For the first time since Tio and Sonja's arrival, Lord Desmos made a comment. "She can handle a sword, Commander, as well as any of your men."

"Indeed," Hubarthis commented, while those flanking him betrayed their doubts in smiles and coughs. Sonja looked at Desmos, but he reached for his wine.

She said quickly, "I was raised by my father, an Hyrkanian soldier, with training equal to any man's." She did not elaborate, knowing that time usually proves the truth of any assertion—just as she had learned, from experience in her earlier years, that a quick temper and show of display often cause more problems than they are worth.

"In any event," Hubarthis continued, "I want to know if either of you, Tio, or Sonja, recognized any of the criminals on board the ship."

"Do you think we'd know them?" Tio asked irritably.

"No, no, of course not. But perhaps if you could describe any of them to us . . . ."

"One of them was huge," Tio answered. "Biggest man I've ever seen in my life. Reddish hair, beard, moustache. He seemed to be the leader."

"There was a woman," Sonja told Hubarthis. "Several, in fact, but one dark-haired woman seemed to stay close by the giant."

"No one else?" Hubarthis inquired.

"We were fighting for our lives," Tio answered curtly, "not taking roll call for a garden party." It seemed to please him to act belligerently to military officers.

"Of course," Hubarthis agreed. A gray-beard seated next to Hubarthis leaned close and whispered in his ear. The commander nodded, and said, "Everyone seems to have noticed the giant man. Did you hear anyone mention the name 'Urdus'?"

"Or 'Urgus' or 'Urthis'," Sonja replied. "Perhaps it was 'Urdus'. They're all common enough names."

"We're asking," Hubarthis told them, "simply because we're trying to figure out who might have been involved."

Tio nodded.

Sonja leaned forward and looked right into Hubarthis' eyes. "There was a sorcerer involved."

"We've heard that, too."

"We weren't close enough to recognize his features, but he was dressed in animal skins."

"You're certain he was a sorcerer?"

"I've had the misfortune to deal with such things," Sonja told him. "He was a sorcerer, all right—and an extremely powerful one."

Hubarthis sighed heavily and sat back, spreading his hands of the table top, his fingertips stretching from the northern to the southern borders on a map of Aquilonia. "Witches and wizards have, of course, been condemned to the Isle," he admitted. "I'm not familiar with sorcery—I've no idea how powerful their spells might have been. Whatever their abilities, we know that they were bound in chains and set ashore there."

"Iron," Sonja told him, "sometimes binds magic. Yet, I don't see how a sorcerer of this power could have been taken in the first place."

"Indeed." Again Hubarthis lifted an eyebrow.

And Sonja thought better of saying anything more about sorcery, lest these militarists decide for themselves that she was a witch.

A bell chimed. Twin doors opened at one end of the hall and a steward, dressed in a white apron, stood back to direct servants into the meeting room. They began to lay down covered silver dishes for the supper. Tio belched, apologized and delightedly took in the aroma of the beef placed before him. Sonja nodded to a servant who poured her wine, then looked again at Desmos, who approached his plate sullenly.

Hubarthis glanced to a marked candle on the table

before him. "Time enough to enjoy your meal," he remarked. "But afterwards, we set sail."

Desmos retired half-way through the course, claiming lack of appetite. When the meal was finished, Tio excused himself and, in the company of a number of Aquilonian troops, made his way down to the galley that would soon set out. A sailor to the core, he wanted to inspect her lines and spit on the deck before pushing from shore.

Hubarthis and his men left to direct the final points of what should be done in the garrison in his absence. And Sonja, her full belly straining her new mail shirt, stepped outside to walk for a moment in the pleasant evening.

The air was warm and the skies cloudless. Birds chirped from trees in the compound courtyard, crowding about the feeding troughs of the horses and those places outside the kitchen where the cooks deposited scraps into a compost pile. Sonja sauntered towards a wood-pile stacked against a great oak tree, with the idea of sitting there for a moment's pause. She was surprised to find there, revealed as a shadow in the twilight, Lord Sir Desmos.

He was sitting beneath the oak, but as soon as Sonja came near he hastily arose and excused himself. But Sonja would not let him pass.

"You didn't say two words at supper," she reminded him, "you, who used to be as garrulous as a minah bird."

He looked beyond her at the thick, night-filled forest behind the garrison walls. "What would you have me say?"

"Nothing in particular. Only whatever the subject might be, make light of it."

Now he looked into her eyes. "The subject is Desmos. How can I make light of myself when I know what I am? I'd feared this—I'd feared it with an ache. I've had nightmares about it . . ."

"That you can't lift a sword?"

"How can I consider myself a man?" He seemed more

to be asking himself than her.

"Sit, Desmos." Sonja placed herself on the log pile. "Sit. Talk."

He leaned uncomfortably against the oak.

"You astonished me, yes," Sonja said, "when I saw you on that ship, frightened as a boy, unable to defend yourself. Yet you told me once that you handled yourself well, and I believe you. What happened?"

Desmos shook his head. "I do not know. I can't tell you. Perhaps it slipped away from me gradually, as I entered more and more into the unreal world of politics. At first I felt no fear of my position. As I sent criminal after criminal to the Isle, I contented myself with knowing that I was their better—that I could meet them on their own terms and best them. Yet I had decided to devote my life to an intangible, to justice. I think I changed gradually. I imagine I was affected by the society I kept, by these dandies for whom the sight of a nosebleed was perilous violence.

"One morning I was in court, passing sentence, ordering that . . . that some dastard be sent in chains to Os Harku, and I looked across at him, and when I met his eyes—I cringed inside. His gaze was steely and hate-filled, and I became ice. He was young, strong, powerful. There was a sneer in his expression which seemed to say that if I—his condemnor—were forced to back my words with action, instead of relying upon society's mob, he would cut me into strips of meat and leave my words of justice as a hollow joke. I was not the same man after that. I turned to drink. I became so morose that my third wife left me, and in turn I devoted myself slavishly to my work. Oh, I tried to prove my valor in practice exhibitions; but the spark was no longer there. I knew the form and the method, but I had lost all heart for it. Time and again, in practice, I allowed myself to be so touched by the dull point; had I been battling for my life, I would have been cut down and left as a ghost. Do you know what that feeling is, Sonja? Do you know what it feels like to hear your younger self pitying you from inside your soul?

"Since then I've been no better than any court dandy. The polite love my little jests and my winsome bon mots; but I detest myself for them. If I could but make one good stroke with a sword again . . ."

He left it unsaid, and fell silent. Sonja watched him.

The clatter of the troops, preparing, sounded from the barracks. Somewhere in the darkness around them two dogs snarled over a scrap of meat. A trumpet blared with the brilliance of a ray of daylight cutting through the dark of night.

"Sword-play isn't everything," Sonja told Desmos after a while. "I live by my sword, true, and I am handy with it—and I know that in the world I tread the sword is the measure of the person. But I also know that in other worlds the sword is nothing; by some the mind is esteemed, and among poets the heart, and with sailors the ability to tack well in a wind. Sometimes these worlds collide. There have been times, on hearing the voice of a good poet or strains of fine music, when I have felt my skill to be a useless, irrelevant thing. In the same way, I'm sure, your voice of justice has meant more than the actions of armed rogues. But where these worlds meet is hazy ground. I have been a criminal, and a poet. You yourself have no doubt done things which, in some other sphere, would be considered crimes. I think you brood too much on something which is of less value than you consider it to be; you wish it, or wish it back, and so it takes on large dimensions. And yet, when you had it, did you give it a second thought?"

"This morning, you might have lost your life. I was not able to aid you when there was need. Had I seen a sword-point at your throat, I would not have had the courage to lift my blade in your defense."

"I believe in fate," said Sonja. "I know I have my own destiny to fulfill, and I have been touched by some of the workings of the world beyond our world. I lived through today, and so did you. Today was not the test; if the test comes to you, Desmos, you will know it. That is when you may praise or damn yourself, according to how you meet it. Until then, learn to live with yourself. Are you sailing with us?"

"Yes. I must." His tone changed. "My brother is on that ship, Sonja. On the *Niros*."

Sonja was surprised. "You know this? Did you see him?"

"I saw a face which I thought his, during the battle. This evening, before supper, I lay down from exhaustion and fell into a half-sleep. I dreamed I saw him again, my brother Betos—mirthless, cruel, wanting to kill me— saw him watching me cower on that ship, and knowing that he had taken a far greater revenge by seeing me helpless than he might have had in slitting my throat." Desmos wrung his hands. "Whether or not he is actually on that ship, whether I have seen or only symbolized him, Betos is there, and I must face him."

Sonja nodded silently.

"I've asked for a sword," Desmos went on. "I'll be given one. No one said anything to Hubarthis about my cowardice. Isn't that strange?"

"Perhaps not," said Sonja. She stood up.

"If I can't kill with it," Desmos assured her, "then I'll kill myself with it."

Sonja shook her head. "Action sometimes must take the place of thought, Desmos. You're thinking, now. Wait till you must act."

"I should have acted today."

"No. You were still thinking today. Even if you'd fought today, you'd still have been thinking."

The horns blew again, stridently this time, calling the troops to formation.

Aleil knocked three times upon the door of the captain's cabin, but heard no response. She paused, then rapped again. Still no answer. From beneath the oak portal she smelled a strange odor—a pungent burning smell, as of fibers or incense . . .

Cautiously, looking behind her shoulder as she did so,

Aleil pressed the latch of Athu's door and pushed it open. She peered in, eased the door open enough to admit herself, and stood on the threshold.

"What do you wish?"

His voice was even and quiet. In the darkness of the cabin, it took Aleil a moment to discover where Athu was located. He had no lamp burning; only the gray, dim light of false dawn filtered through the grilled porthole above his bunk. As her eyes grew accustomed to the dimness, Aleil saw the wizard sitting cross-legged on a mat in the center of the floor. Before him, on a tripod originally designed for holding a wine flask, stood a small clay bowl which glowed and smoked. Incense, Aleil decided—but its perfume was far from delightful.

She approached the Shemite cautiously, her bare feet whispering on the wood. When she stood before him, she paused a moment, then sat down facing him, crossing her legs like his.

"I thought you might be asleep," she whispered.

"I am not."

"I smelt the burning of the incense, and was afraid that a candle might have overturned."

"I am concentrating. Why have you come?"

She could feel his piercing eyes locating her through the darkness. They actually seemed to glow with a faint light. "I—I wanted to talk to you."

"Speak, then."

Aleil looked at him uneasily. "I'm taking a chance in coming here, you know. If Urdus found out, he'd probably cut my throat. Yours, too."

"Do you think I fear Urdus?"

"No . . ." Her voice was uncertain.

"Tell me why you've come here."

Aleil swallowed with difficulty, partly because of the pungent incense fumes. "I—I wanted to see you, Athu, because—you interest me. Maybe I'm attracted to you."

"You never felt that way on the Isle."

Aleil shrugged. "But we escaped yesterday. Isn't that strange? I don't think we could have done it if it hadn't been for your sorcery."

"That's very true. Is that why you're suddenly attracted to me?"

Aleil purred a laugh; with slim gray fingers she plucked at the ragged edge of her skirt. In the bare light of the refracted moon her eyes were pools of darkness and her lips two full lines of shimmering brightness. She leaned forward, so that her features were quietly touched by the orange radiance of the incense coals. "I was sentenced to the Isle for practicing witchcraft," she said.

"Indeed."

"Well, that and murder."

"Ah."

"I know spells and potions and poison dolls," she went on matter-of-factly, "—although, in truth, perhaps my finest accomplishments have been achieved by use of my woman's wiles."

"You said you wished to speak to me, Aleil, yet you have not told me anything. Are you attracted to my sorcery? Do you think to make use of it?"

Again she purred a throaty laugh.

"You read me well, Athu. Now that we've escaped the Isle, there's no telling what may happen. I'm frightened of what lies ahead—and I'm frightened of Urdus, too. He seems to think that we'll continue together, he and I, and live in Aquilonia. But I want no part of him.

"He was of use to you on the Isle," said Athu.

"Aye—but I want to be free when we get to shore."

"So now you wish to make use of me."

"I want your protection, Athu. I can make it—rewarding—for you."

"With your woman's wiles?"

"You'd find me a stimulating companion. Even Shemitish sorcerers, I imagine, like a woman's company from time to time. Wasn't that so, back there on the Isle? I think you wanted me, and I know Urdus thought so. Believe me when I say I want to be done with him. I can keep you alert to what he is thinking and doing, and—"

"And in return, all you wish of me is protection?"

"Yes. And, perhaps, some lessons in magic."

"No. No training in magic. My powers were given to me by monstrous beings, and cannot be imparted to others."

Aleil noticed again, with some uneasiness, the spectral glow in the sorcerer's eyes.

"In any case," Aleil said, "I can trust you, can't I?"

"To the same degree that I can trust you, or that you can trust yourself."

Aleil grinned and stood up. "I'd better be going. It's almost dawn, and Urdus is a light sleeper."

"Go, then."

"One last thing, Athu. What is the secret of your blood-work?"

The wizard shook his head, warningly.

"That box . . . ?"

Athu looked up at her. "So soon you begin? You have given me nothing, yet you ask so much?"

"I'm—curious."

"We are all curious," Athu replied. "All humans are curious. Perhaps that is why we all became damned souls."

Urdus awoke at the first light of dawn, having slept only fitfully for the few hours he had allowed himself. He was surprised not to find Aleil beside him. Grumbling over her absence, he rose from his berth, quickly swallowed half a cup of wine to bolster himself, dressed, and strapped his longsword about his waist.

In the corridor he found one of his worthies standing guard outside his door.

"They're still at it, Urdus."

"Oh?" It was more a growl than a query.

"Now they're casting dice."

"Damn 'em," Urdus grumbled, and made his way up the stairs.

Prowling the poop-deck, he found a knot of men

hunched against the port bulkhead. The steersman warily eyed the giant. Beyond the larboard rail, an orange sun was rising slowly above the Aquilonian forest.

"What now?" Urdus demanded, striding near the group and then standing with fists on hips.

Most of the men rose and backed away, but one remained seated, one hand on his wine-cup, the other tapping the deck beside a pair of dice. He was not large, but was lean and hard, with a wiry muscularity that suggested quickness.

"We're debating," he told Urdus without looking up at him.

"Debating?" growled Urdus. "That's almost a step up from quarreling. You're becoming civilized, Otos."

"Mitra strike me!" the ruffian cried, throwing back his head. "We're evenly divided, Urdus; half of us wish to remain on your course, the others of us have decided to tack about and head north."

Urdus looked to his pilot. "You've stayed on course downstream?" he demanded.

Otos spoke for the man. "He hasn't steered one wave's-breadth from your directions, Urdus, though I doubt we've gained even one league by it. An accursed wind has been against us!"

"So you want to sail north, Otos? There are dinghys aboard. You're welcome to one of them."

"Dinghys!" Otos rose to his feet. "I'm telling you there's an ill wind against us. We own this ship as well as you, Urdus. All of us took it, not you alone!"

Urdus approached him. The others stepped back. But Otos met the huge man's stare without flinching.

"*I* led the charge," Urdus told him coldly. "*I* made the plan and *I* took the ship. If you don't want to obey me, you should have told me before you came aboard. As long as my sword is at my side, *I* run the ship. Is that understood?"

Otos had no chance to reply. Suddenly, from above, ringing crisply through the dawn air, came the cry of the man in the lookout nest. "Galley to the north!"

Urdus tossed back his red-brown mane of hair. "Can you make 'er out?"

"Aquilonian—a military galleass!"

"Damn it!" Otos raged. "I knew we should have chased after those survivors! Now they've brought the troops down on us!"

Urdus turned on him and held up a fist. "You'll fight them!" he snarled. "All you dogs'll fight them!" He spotted the dice on the deck and savagely kicked them away. "And after we've beaten them, *then* we'll have another throw of the dice!"

Otos glowered at him, but did not reply.

"Now, all of you get down from here! To your posts!"

They went—sullenly, some of them, and others briskly.

Aleil came up the way as the criminals departed. "Where have you been?" Urdus asked her.

"Taking air. I couldn't sleep. It was stifling . . . ."

He sneered, then ignored her and looked up to his man in the nest. "What's she making?" he called out.

"She's overtaking us! She'll be on us before long. Those bastards can haul oar when they want to."

Urdus growled and pushed Aleil aside, made his way down into the mid-deck. Then he paused, eying a man who was sitting on a keg whittling at a design on a knife handle: two gryphons engaged claw-to-claw in cherry wood.

"What about you?" Urdus asked him.

The man looked up; his face was lean, scarred, bitter. "I'm with you, Urdus, as always. You know that. I've wanted to kill Aquilonians far too long to back down from it now."

"Aye." Urdus smiled grimly. "You've been my right-hand man, Betos, and I trust you above all others. Stand with me but once more."

The giant Vanir walked on. Betos continued with his whittling, which was made more difficult by the fact that he was missing two fingers from his left hand.

Chapter 5

There was an Aquilonian proverb: Even the fleetest fox cannot run all day under a hot sun.

Captain Hubarthis thought of this as his galley drew close upon the *Niros*. Aye—but a fox *would* run, despite the likelihood of capture. Why, then, had this one dallied just off the western shore of Os Harku, rather than fleeing downriver? There had been a good, favoring wind . . .

The sun was now well up. Hubarthis and those near him on the bow could even make out the sheen of sweat on the faces of those criminals staring at them, just ahead. They saw Urdus, the giant Vanir warrior, standing straight and tall and scowling on the poop of the *Niros,* staring as the Aquilonians bore down.

Hubarthis made a signal. "Get ready."

His soldiers bristled against the gunwales, standing solidly with drawn swords or strung bows or lifted axes. Grappling lines were being readied. Hubarthis had never attempted this tactic before—but then never before, to his knowledge, had any criminals captured a ship to escape from the Isle. He had read battle reports and had talked to men who had engaged with pirates on the waters. It had always struck Hubarthis as an undesirable form of battle. How to use ships the way one uses a horse, or even a battalion? Yet now, as the moments came down, he found himself enjoying the strategic challenge, and consciously admiring those naval officers who could make war in this manner.

Hubarthis lifted his right hand.

His troops readied for the first blow. Bows lifted; swords quivered. A few men spat into the wind for luck.

They could hear breezes whistling through the *Niros'* cordage, booming upon her pennants and full sails. The spray of the *Niros'* wake misted the air before the Aquilonians.

Sonja, Desmos and Tio stood just behind Hubarthis, all with naked swords in their hands, silent.

Hubarthis held his hand steady. The gold embroidery on his gloves winked in the bright sunlight.

Aboard the *Niros,* Urdus' men stood packed and hushed, waiting for the assault. In the middeck stood Aleil, and beside her Athu. Somehow she sensed that the sorcerer had no intention of using his power to aid Urdus.

Behind them, by the way to the poop, were Otos and those who had sided with him against the Vanir. Urdus sensed Otos' angry glare burning into his back, even as he felt Captain Hubarthis' steely stare confronting him across the short space of waves. Urdus saw the lifted Aquilonian bows; his own men lifted theirs. He saw the notched axes and the straight swords, and knew that behind him his men, too, stood ready with ax and sword. He knew he need not be concerned with Otos' possible mutiny; the dog would fight for his life with the rest.

Urdus stared hard at Hubarthis, and ached to meet the man in combat.

Hubarthis lowered his hand.

A cloud of arrows arced shallowly and sped towards the *Niros.*

Urdus' men fell back, crude shields up as the shafts dropped; untrained, they shuffled and moved, pushed one another out of the way. Arrows punched through the canvas of the sails, dug into the timber of the decks and masts, splashed into the waters. Some men screamed, feathered through their chests or throats.

Hubarthis raised his right hand again. "Ready second volley!"

In that instant Urdus made a rash act, an act of insanity, an act of desperation and courage.

As the first of the arrows fell upon his decks he whirled and shoved his steersman from the wheel, grabbed the spokes and with a mighty effort swung the *Niros* about in a ninety degree curve. His men howled as they were thrown off their feet.

Urdus lashed the wheel and turned again, held out his sword and planted his feet to the deck. To his reeling sight the Aquilonian galley veered off to starboard but still came on, then straightened and headed hungrily, squarely for the barge's mid-hull.

"Ready to board them!" he roared.

Otos, clinging to the rail, turned on him. "Are you mad? They'll *ram* us!"

Hubarthis was howling to his steersman, but it was far too late to veer away. Within instants the dragon prowed Aquilonian rose and fell, seemed to take aim upon the *Niros'* pitching side, and rammed her.

Otos lurched up the way, grabbed Urdus' arm as the ship shuddered violently. "You're mad!" he screamed.

Urdus laughed in his face. "I've turned 'er about! Now if you want to live—all of you dogs—*take that ship!*"

Tio bawled in agony as the trireme struck the *Niros*.

The sharp dragon-prow bit into the hull and splintered, and on both ships men were thrown from their feet. Masts creaked, sails ripped, men howled. Urdus, hanging onto the rail, held his sword up and laughed like a maniac. Gigantic sprays of river-water foamed up, and the criminals shrieked like damned souls as the *Niros* began to fill quickly.

"Take their ship!" Urdus howled savagely. "Take it, if you want to *live!*" And even as he yelled he boarded the galley the only way possible—over the dragon's head prow. The giant raced to the mid-deck where men lay disabled, where wood was shattered and cordage blew loose, where the broken bodies of Aquilonians lay flung in tumbled heaps.

In the midst of the Shirki the two ships revolved in the current, the pleasure barge sinking, sails flapping, as the men aboard her swarmed to the attack.

Hubarthis, Sonja, Desmos and Tio had nearly been thrown into the river. They were half crushed by the bodies of the soldiers behind them. Now thunder seemed to surround them all as the frenzied criminals leapt roaring upon the Aquilonian war-ship in a frantic effort to save themselves from death. They pulled themselves erect, and Hubarthis gasped, "Madmen! Fools!"

But there was no time for talk. The Aquilonian foredeck was already a heap of bodies. Sonja staggered, fell back against the rail as the first wave of criminals, howling and waving steel, surged to the assault. They did not pause on the foredeck but plowed through the scattered bodies to attack the stunned Aquilonians, making way for others behind them with grappling hooks and chains.

Another wave came, and another. Hubarthis was up, and Tio, and all their men. The first deafening clatter of swords filled the air.

The *Niros* groaned almost humanly, and the men still aboard her shrieked and cried out. She rolled lopsided as she filled with river water; her mainmast creaked and swayed dangerously.

Desmos was clambering away on hands and knees, awkwardly dragging his sword with him in his right hand. He was pushed or booted and sent sprawling before Sonja's feet. Sonja yelled at him; she moved with sword out, and a splash of blood dropped into Desmos' hair. Quickly he pulled himself erect, his left hand behind him and grasping the rail. His eyes were wide.

A rushing wave of strife and death surged up before him: soldiers and convicts—swords and axes—tromping

boots and glittering armor—cries, shrieks and moans—
bloody faces clawed by bloody hands—struggling bodies, backs, shoulders and arms—

Sonja faced him for an instant. "Act! Act *now*,
Desmos!"

Then she threw herself into the fray.

"My ship!" Tio was howling maniacally, swinging his
sword with all his strength. "My ship!" A snarling ruffian came towards him with lifted blade and Tio had at
him furiously, cleaving him from flank to spine.

Captain Hubarthis and those other Aquilonians near
Tio—those who had not fallen or been slain on the
foredeck with the first crash of the ships—stood in a
circle, fending off the wave of attackers who ringed them
round. Each time one of them fell they pulled back and
closed ranks, offering a wall of flashing swords and axes
to the renegades. Blades clashed and rang together, spitting blue sparks. The heavy chopping sounds of steel
cutting through flesh and bone mingled with howls of
utter agony.

Sonja worked more in the open, as was her preference
—wheeling, running, crouching, attacking wherever she
saw a chance. Jumping from the foredeck, she met the
blades of three startled criminals. The first went down
with a split head, the second with blood spouting from
the stump of an arm. The third sought to press her back
to the stairs, where the piling carcasses and running
blood would trip and confuse her—

But Sonja's blade worked like a living thing; a whirl of
silver, constantly spinning, arcing, pressing. When she
slipped on a thick trail of blood, she instinctively threw
herself sidewise, and her opponent's sword bit heavily
into the wooden stairs. It took him but an instant to
work it free, but in that brief time Sonja pushed herself
up, feeling her left arm sink to the wrist in the mush of
dead man's slashed belly. She clamped her fist,
furiously threw a long line of running entrails full into
her attacker's face. He yelled and dropped back. Sonja

leaped up and clove him sidewise through the rib-cage.

She heard a scream behind her, wheeled and looked.

It was Desmos again, cowered against the rail as a huge brute came at him awkwardly with an axe. The nobleman was trying to lift his blade in any sort of defense, but it was as if his muscles had gone numb. The renegade with the axe saw his opponent's fear, and laughed. One boot clamped down on Desmos' sword, holding it to the deck. Desmos lifted his free arm to his face. The dog lifted his axe.

"Fight!" Sonja screamed—but was unheard above the din.

The axe descended—

Then suddenly, from the blurred mob behind, a sword moved out and lopped off the hand, which spun free on a gusher of blood, still gripping the axe. The sword returned to its business within the mob; the axe-man shrieked and tripped backwards. Sonja briefly glimpsed the swordsman—a man with a lean, scarred face, who was already engaged in fighting another Aquilonian within the melee.

Before she could puzzle over why one of the criminals would deliberately smite another, she saw a shadow behind her. She ducked and leapt forward, towards the stairs. A hiss, a whoosh, as something whipped the air just above her head. She pivoted, sword up, and as her assailant doubled back, straining, she jumped, skewering him through the heart.

No one else stood nearby. Panting, she looked back at Desmos. He was on his feet, holding his sword above him, two-handed. Before him, crouched on the deck, sat the axe-man, cursing, trying to stop the blood from spouting from his severed wrist.

Desmos shrieked furiously and brought down the sword. There was a splatter of blood, bits of bone and hair. The axe-man fell lopsided, cut perfectly through the head, the sword having passed down into the chest and almost out the side.

Desmos fell back against the rail. Sonja saw tears in his eyes.

"Desmos!"

He looked at her, saw her, stared at her with tears running down his cheeks and a white grimace showing through his beard.

Sonja left him, ran farther down into the mid-deck.

Swords flashed, men screamed. Blood and bodies were everywhere—heads—mangled and dismembered limbs—wounded and groaning victims—and still the swords clattered.

She saw a giant bespattered with running crimson, standing his ground and sweeping his sword in wide circles, roaring Vanirian war-cries. There were others beside Urdus, and together they fought with desperate fury against the crowd of Aquilonians who surged against them.

Sonja ran towards the poop, but a scattered ring of criminals held her back. One rushed in and engaged her, while Aquilonian soldiers moved in and around, hacking and thrusting, unable to form ranks for defense. From above, a renegade with a knife suddenly swung down on a line and thrust at Sonja's face; she sensed his wild tactic barely in time, dipped and brought up her sword. The ruffian flew, shrieking, through the air, letting go the line, as blood gushed out his front from breastbone to groin.

Where Hubarthis and Tio fought, another Aquilonian went down—and another. Their dwindling knot of defense provided a target for the criminals.

A scream, and still another fell—a young man whose parents Hubarthis knew well. Enraged, the captain sought to avenge the murder; his blade slashed into a scalp and the killer fell back shrieking; but Hubarthis' sudden action confused Tio, who was duelling a lean, rat-faced man armed with a pike. Tio missed his mark, stumbled—and the pike slammed through his belly.

"Good stroke, Otos!" yelled another rogue.

Howling in a last frenzy before death took hold, Tio lifted his sword and smote with all his might—but Otos, laughing, nimbly withdrew. Tio coughed and sobbed as he went down, bleeding, onto a pile of fresh bodies, where he writhed in torment. With the last of his vision he saw the battered sleeve of some mail-armor gleam and fade and blur.

Sonja fought on—but she saw fewer and fewer Aquilonians now. Before her, on the poop, Urdus hacked away the armored head of some soldier, and no one else rose up against him.

"Sorcery protects him!" she heard a soldier cry out. "Steel will not come near his body—!"

Urdus laughed hugely. The men beside the giant lifted their bloody swords high and began cheering.

Sonja heard more cheers answering from the foredeck.

Then, before her, a rowdy ring of bloody renegades formed a wall—seven of them, ranged in a line—and faced her. Sonja's nostrils flared.

She glanced up as Urdus' voice boomed loudly: "Take captives! Take captives!"

Footsteps behind her—she whirled cat-like, on instinct, and another renegade went down, cut squarely across the throat. But no more behind him—only piles and piles of the dead, still dripping . . .

And before her, the approaching wall of angry faces and red-smeared swords and axes.

"Put down your blade!" snarled one of them.

"Dog! We'll both be in Hell before I'll put down this blade!" She lifted her sword.

"No, Sonja. . . ."

She half-pivoted, saw Desmos—blood on his arms face and hair, but swordless. His arms were behind him and he was escorted by a gang of crimson-spattered convicts.

"Desmos!"

"Hubarthis is giving it up, Sonja. They'll take u alive . . ."

"Dogs!" Sonja howled.

They jumped for her. She knocked aside two swords, dropped back, met a third and blocked it, wheeled her blade to guard against a fourth and fifth. Bootsteps sounded behind her; Sonja whirled, jumped and thrust —but the renegade held back.

Sonja backed against the gunwale, snarling fiercely, malevolence in her sparking sapphire eyes. She lifted her sword and fixed her lips in a feral grin. "Come ahead!" she hissed. "I promise you entry to the Hells before I draw my last breath!"

The men hesitated; hardened felons though they were, this savage woman's fury gave them pause.

Then a huge face appeared behind the seven—Urdus. Sonja glowered at him. The giant laughed.

Behind him, down into the mid-deck, came a slow-moving crowd—the last of the pirates still alive, perhaps thirty of them, bringing as prisoners the few weaponless and war-stained Aquilonians: Hubarthis, and eight of his men.

"Come ahead!" Sonja yelled. "Dogs! Pigs! I never throw down my sword—*never! Come ahead!*"

Silence answered her. No man lifted a blade.

Sonja's angry eyes roved over all the renegades—over Desmos, Hubarthis and his men, all bound—and re-alized with a cold stillness in her heart that the battle was over, that she was cornered and could not kill them all.

A numbness stole over her.

"Erlik's tongue . . ." she whispered.

Hubarthis shook his head. "Give it up, Sonja. This way we may live . . ."

"Fool!" she yelled at him. "Coward! Aquilonian!" She cursed him with his nationality as if it were a damn-ing epithet.

The line parted, and the giant stepped through. Silent-ly, eyes full upon Sonja, he stepped towards her. The sword in his hand was huge, blood-stained, but he did not lift it as for a duel. Instead he held it out, point down, then thrust it into the deckboards. The fresh blood upon it ran down the length of the blade and collected in a small pool on the boards.

Sonja sneered.

Urdus stepped past it and held out his hand. "Give me the sword."

Sonja's breath went shallow. She could not swallow. She looked sharply to Hubarthis. "Damn you!" she spat.

Hubarthis shook his head, as if she were very wrong.

Urdus kept his hand out.

Slowly, slowly, Sonja lowered her point, her hand trembling as if resisting a compelling force.

She sensed the presence of sorcery.

The blade touched the deck.

Dozens of faces stared at her, while she wondered at herself—cursed herself.

The *Niros,* its timbers toppled, began at last to go under.

And Sonja stared in disbelief as two figures lifted from the decks of the ill-fated barge and floated through the air: a dark-bearded man dressed in a robe of animal skins, bearing a raven-tressed woman in his arms. His barbaric robe fluttered in the air as he carried the woman above the river, above the two ships, and brought her and himself gently to rest upon the poop deck of the Aquilonian galley.

"Mitra!" Sonja exclaimed under her breath. She realized that this man, not Urdus, was the cause of the subtle force that was immobilizing her. Then Urdus stepped ahead and took her sword from her hand, and Sonja let him.

Urdus threw her sword behind him without looking to see where it fell. Still his gaze lingered on her, and he grimaced a smile. Sonja glared at him. Her crimson hair, blood-spattered, rose and fell upon her shoulders, blew about her face.

"Good. You are wise," Urdus rumbled.

Sonja stared up at him. The barbaric Vanir was at least a full head taller than she.

"Chain them up!" Urdus ordered. He waved, and five of his tribe surrounded Sonja. She was quickly ushered to where the other prisoners were gathered in the mid deck. Urdus yelled for men to take axes and free the galleass from the sinking *Niros*.

Down the stairs from the poop deck came Athu with Aleil—Athu and his cedar box trimmed with bronze and copper. Urdus cast him a sidelong glance. Slowly the wizard made his way around the decks, stealing misty crimson vapor from the corpses before they were thrown over into the jaws of the crocodiles and serpents.

The eleven captives watched him, half-mesmerised, feeling astonishment and a strange lack of will.

As they were made to stand under guard, one of Urdus' men came forward to stare at them. He was blood-stained and spattered with gore; he carried his notched sword in a weary right hand, and his left was missing two fingers. Sonja suddenly recognized him as the swordsman who had saved Desmos from death.

For a long moment he stood and stared at all the prisoners, but especially at Desmos. The nobleman kept his head bent low, and only when he felt the force of the man's intense gaze did he suddenly look up—to stare into eyes very like his own.

Betos laughed mirthlessly. "Greetings, O brother. Did you think I would let you die?"

Desmos groaned.

"Thank me, Desmos. I have saved your life. How many nights I've lain awake, praying to the Lords of the Hells for such a moment as this? And now it has come."

Desmos looked away, looked back—horrified, anguished.

"My beloved, self-righteous brother," Betos said, clucking his tongue against his teeth. "The judge. You have come to me at last!"

*   *   *

The damaged galley could not travel far. Urdus sailed her as well as he could manage, but the craft would not respond fully to the wheel. There were not enough men remaining to make turns at the three tiers of oars effective—not enough men, in fact, to both row and guard the captives simultaneously—so Urdus did the best he could, piloting the trireme down the main current and guiding it with difficulty towards the near shore.

The shore of Aquilonia?

In the quiet of late afternoon the galley skimmed along the shoreline, and with a turn of the spokes Urdus brought it to a jolting stop upon the riverbank. The huge ship crunched into roots and rocks, and nearly spun around; its tall masts splintered and tangled in overhanging limbs; its hull groaned and quivered as it scraped along the embankment.

"Drop anchors!" Urdus ordered his men. "Lash the ship as best you can to trees and boulders." Then he took charge of escorting the eleven captives ashore.

Whether by chance or design, Urdus' laborious navigation had brought him to a fortuitous harbor. The riverbank rose steeply, through thick brush and clogged forest, to an outcropping of rocks. Immediately east, beyond the lush forest at the river's edge, rose nearly sheer prominences and cliffs pocked with caves and delves. Urdus led his company toward them.

The Aquilonian captives, Sonja among them, were tied together in a long line, bound crudely but securely with chains and ropes. They did not speak much. On the painful journey through the forest towards the caves, Urdus' men and women gathered fruit and filled their animal skins with water from streams. Two or three lucky arrows brought down fowl, to be roasted later.

Once during the march, Aleil approached Athu and whispered hurriedly into his ear, "Why did you deliver the red-haired woman into Urdus' hands?"

"Because there is something strange about her sword skill, almost a magical quality. She might have slain him."

Aleil pondered. "Did you also, then, cast a sorcerous glamor about him in battle, so that the Aquilonians could not touch him?"

"Aye."

"I thought—"

Athu smiled darkly. "I do not aid him, nor his enemies. His schemes mean nothing to me. I care only that he shall not die before the time of my own choosing."

Aleil sensed that she would learn no more from the wizard. She walked silently away from him, noticing with some anxiousness that Urdus was scowling darkly at her.

Dusk was deepening when they at last reached the hillside and began to prepare camp. Urdus ordered a large circle to be cleared upon a flat stretch of rocky land situated before the highest accessible cliff. His men did as directed, clearing away scrub, digging fire pits, collecting boulders and big logs for seats. They lit tinder with flint and steel, began roasting their few caught fowl and some of the fruit over flames. Urdus relaxed somewhat, seeing that all his companions followed his orders. Even Otos seemed tolerant of Urdus taking charge— Otos and the handful of belligerents who shared his temper.

Sonja, Captain Hubarthis, Desmos and their fellow captives were deposited in the center of the clearing. Their chains were not removed, but Urdus had Aleil and another woman give them water, and announced that they would be fed when he and his companions had supped. The Vanir warrior stood proudly before his captives as he spoke, the firelight playing around him.

"You've sent other patrols after us, Captain Hubarthis?"

Hubarthis raised his head fiercely, meeting Urdus' proud sneer as strongly as he was able. "Another ship sailed. Why are you keeping us alive?"

"N6 land patrols? Surely you sent land patrols."

"It doesn't matter. Why are you keeping us alive?" Hubarthis demanded again.

"Because I am certain you have sent land patrols. And if they find us, they'll act friendlier if they know we have men of such distinction held under our swords."

"They'd attack just the same. We are all expendable."

"I think not." Urdus turned from him, faced Desmos. "So you are Betos' famous brother?"

Desmos looked up briefly, looked away.

"Are you deaf? Was your tongue cut out during the battle?"

Still Desmos did not answer; his face flushed, apparent even in the dim firelight.

Urdus showed his teeth; he kicked Desmos savagely on the soles of his feet.

Sonja writhed in her bonds. "Leave him alone!" she spat.

Urdus turned to her. "Ah, yes." He smiled grimly. "You—the red-haired one. What are you, his wife?"

"I'm no one's wife."

The Vanir regarded Sonja more closely. "You're not even Aquilonian. And you fought like a tigress. What're you doing with these weaklings parading as men?"

Sonja looked full up into Urdus' face; her cheeks moved; Urdus' eyes narrowed. An instant too late he thought of drawing back. Then Sonja spat full into his eyes.

The giant jerked away growling and wiped his brows, then brought his hand down in a sweep. Sonja avoided the blow with perfect timing, throwing herself back just beyond Urdus' reach, feeling the wind of his moving hand. Urdus snarled, sensing eyes at the cooking fires turned towards him. He bent closer to Sonja and with both hands grabbed her hair, pulled her face toward him.

"Vixen!"

Sonja moved again, this time forward. With the quickness of a viper she clamped her teeth upon Urdus' lower lip and held onto it. The giant howled. Blood spurted.

From behind, Aleil laughed.

Urdus clamped his fists to Sonja's head, pressed his knuckles against her temples until she gasped and let go of him. Urdus threw her back; Sonja took down the two men chained on either side of her as she fell upon the ground. Quickly she straightened and sat up again, her lips skewed into a vicious red snarl. Urdus' blood was salty on her tongue, and it dripped down one side of her chin.

Urdus wiped at his swelling lip, examined the blood on his fingers. "Bitch!" he yelled, and stood for a moment, eyes blazing furiously, bent over Sonja, fists clenched to pummel her—

But something held him back.

Something in the red-haired woman's sapphire eyes, blazing as fiercely as his own? Some mockery, some recognition of equality, some threat of vengeance?

"No, bitch, you'll not die just yet—nor so quickly."

Urdus straightened himself; the hint of a brutal smile played behind his beard, and he turned from Sonja and the other captives, strode toward his own fire, where Betos was roasting one of the birds.

Aleil could not restrain herself—perhaps because Athu, the sorcerer, stood silent and grim beside her. Whatever the reason, she spoke before she thought, yelling after the Vanir, "What, Urdus? Does she not kiss well enough for you?"

The camp fell silent, all eyes watching Urdus. He turned and faced Aleil.

Athu felt the woman begin to tremble.

Urdus returned towards her with a measured tread. Aleil swallowed; she fell back a pace. Urdus came up and stood before her, devouring her with his baleful stare.

"Are you now so brave," he asked in a dark whisper, "with this Shemite sorcerer so near by you? Is that it, Aleil? Have you given up your common sense for him? Heh? Perhaps you no longer eat food, Aleil—perhaps you'd rather suck blood, like this sorcerer!"

Aleil was trembling terribly. Athu, next to her, showed no emotion whatsoever.

Urdus' arm suddenly lashed out; one huge hand grabbed Aleil's dark hair. The woman squealed. Urdus turned and dragged her beside him towards the ring of captives.

All the others stood up or came close to observe. Betos watched somberly from his post. Otos' rat-face shimmered with perspiration in the flickering firelight; he licked his lips.

"Suck it, then, Aleil!" Urdus growled, and with one arm forced her to crouch before Sonja.

Sonja glared at him, astonished. Before she could manage to move, Urdus pushed Aleil's face into hers, forced Aleil's lips to Sonja's, with one hand ground Aleil's mouth into the blood on Sonja's lips.

Aleil fought back, crying and writhing to be free.

Urdus laughed, pushed her head the harder.

Then Sonja kicked her feet and backed off, spat on the ground and called Urdus obscenities.

Urdus howled with laughter and drew Aleil to her feet by her hair, then slammed her sprawling back on the ground with a casual surge of strength. Aleil landed on her butt and fell back; her head hit the hard ground, one of her ankle bracelets broke and one of her rounded breasts fell free. Sobbing and wailing, she pulled herself up, kicked away the pebble bracelet, wrapped her tunic around her bared breast and, covering her face with her hands, limped away from the fires.

Passing Athu, she punched him roughly on the shoulder, disgusted with him. The wizard stood silent, unmoved.

Urdus watched her go. As the woman disappeared into a shadowed knot of trees, where her fading sobs continued to trail from her, he turned to a man at a fire.

"Take this one." He pointed at Sonja. "Chain her to a tree over there. No food."

Sonja called him names. Urdus turned from her and went to his fire.

But Sonja did not fight with the man as he separated her from the others and led her away. Someone else rejoined the chains and rope between the two that had flanked her.

Sonja was chained just within the perimeter of campfire light, and there she sat, crouching awkwardly, watching as the Aquilonians were fed and given water. After a while she turned her face from them and tried to get some sleep. Her body was utterly fatigued and sore. Slight wounds she had suffered made themselves felt in proportion as she relaxed and allowed rest to overtake her. And her belly growled.

Aleil finally slunk back towards the campfires when the Aquilonians had been fed. There were only a few pieces of fruit left; she chewed on one of these, sitting by herself on a rock away from the campfires.

Athu, too, kept to himself, in the darkness outside the camp perimeter.

Urdus assigned men to stand watch. All fires but one were put out. The night settled down to the sounds of a low-blowing wind and the peripheral noise of buzzing insects.

In the middle of the night, when all the camp but the guards had fallen asleep, Athu the Shemite took his wooden box and began wandering through the woods. So silent was he that he did not even disturb the owls and nightbirds with his passage.

After a time he found the waterfall and the pool he knew so well, and set down his cedar-wood box. And there, under the brilliant patchy moonlight of the forest, he began the preliminaries of a strange work, scooping up clay and mud from the margin of the pool and carrying it up into the cave that formed the left eye of Swordskull.

Chapter 6

Sonja awoke instantly at the sound of footsteps, leaned her head back against the hard bark of the oak tree and let her eyes rove in all directions. It felt like it was nearly dawn; there was a faint lightening of the sky behind her, which differentiated the sleeping figures in the camp. None of the guards was awake; their exertions of the previous day had whittled down their energy, and now they slumped against rocks or sprawled on the perimeters of the encampment, drowsing.

Only one figure moved, and Sonja watched him as he approached.

Otos.

He crept as quietly as he could towards Sonja. Circling around the sleeping figures, he approached her from her left, holding a finger to his lips as a gesture for silence. Guardedly she watched him. Otos squatted down before her, eying her keenly. Then from his vest he drew out an apple—rather fresh, and not one that had been roasted over a fire. He held it out for Sonja, put it to her lips; she opened her mouth and took a bite, chewed while keeping her eyes on the renegade. When she had eaten the apple entirely, she finally spoke.

"Why do you bring me food?" Her voice was a whisper in the dimness.

"I knew you must be hungry."

"What do you care?" Her attitude was one of total mistrust.

Otos grinned; his eyes were brutal, calculating. "I think we can help one another, you and I."

"Doing what?"

Otos bent closer. "You want to be free. I've seen how you handle a sword, and I know you hate Urdus. We can help one another."

"You'll set me free?"

"Perhaps . . ."

"In return for what?"

"You are not the only one here who hates Urdus. Many of us do also. But more side with him. Urdus won't let any of us go our own way until he gives the word. He fears Aquilonian troops, and will need as many swords as he can muster if a patrol shows up. But I can't see the sense in staying with him."

"Then why don't you just run off?"

"Because *I* might run straight into the lap of a patrol, myself. Can't have that. But if my men and I freed you and your friends—then we could all escape together. If we came across any Aquilonian soldiers, you could explain to them what had happened—or at least offer enough of a defense for us to get away in time. Or, we could—"

Sonja sneered. "You haven't thought this out very well, have you?"

Otos made a grumbling sound in his throat. "I've thought a lot about *you,* though."

"Dog!" Sonja spat. "That's all you want me for, is it?"

Otos grinned more widely. He came closer to Sonja, leering brutishly, reached out and stroked her hair, held her head. Sonja shook his hands away.

"Fool!" Otos whispered to her tautly. "How proud you are in chains, you fiery slut! Yet, I can help you get away."

"Go fry in the Hells!"

Otos stood up, glared down at her. "Whore! I can do what I want with you—you're a prisoner. Remember that. You spit in my face like you did to Urdus and I'll make sure you die in those chains! Think about it. I'll be back."

That said, he half-turned to leave her, took a step. Sonja twisted in her bonds and slid on the ground, kicked out and caught Otos' boots, tripping him and sending him sprawling.

"Dog!" she howled at the top of her voice. "Cursed of Tarim! Get away from me!"

Instantly the camp came alive as sleepy guards leaped up from their cold fires and stared at them.

Otos, half-lying on the gravel, showed a face of wide eyed shock to Sonja, who continued yelling.

"Son of a dog! Brother to Ilmet's serpent! Get away, or I'll kick your manhood into your stomach! Pig! Dog!"

Urdus' growl sounded like a rumble of thunder on a distant horizon. Hurried bootsteps carried throughout the camp, and before Otos could rise he was pulled to his feet by Urdus' massive strength.

"What the hell is going on?"

Otos squirmed in the giant's grasp, but to no avail. Urdus held on to Otos' tunic.

"This dog tried to rape me!" Sonja spat.

"Thing!" Urdus roared in contempt. "Serpent! Lizard!" He shook the renegade violently, then flung Otos from him. The rat-faced man hit the ground, tumbled and rolled, came up crouching with his back against a tall rock.

Urdus drew his sword, took three steps toward the small, wiry criminal. "Shall I exact my punishment, Otos?" he roared, pointing his blade at the man's crotch.

Otos fisted and unfisted his hands, his nostrils flaring, breeches and tunic torn, eyes glaring with hate and fear.

"No . . ." he croaked finally.

"Then get back with the others!"

Otos slunk warily back to the awakened camp, while Urdus watched him. The the giant turned again to Sonja and licked his swollen, purpling underlip. He smiled cruelly, letting his eyes linger over her. Sonja's eyes met his, but there was no attraction in his eyes, no gratitude or appreciation in hers—only a dark, mutual communication of hate between the two.

Urdus turned on his heel and scabbarded his sword. "Get up, all of you!" he yelled, clapping his hands loudly. He surveyed his motley troop, most of them already fully awake. Then he strode to his campfire, looked down at the stirring renegades, and addressed them.

"We move to a higher ground, up the mountainside. We'll stay together until we are well away from the shoreline. If we cross any patrols, we fight." His scornful glare studied every face below him. "Now, gather up your things."

The convicts did as Urdus commanded, and the prisoners were hauled to their feet. As the camp prepared to remove, Betos took a moment to speak with his brother.

"Did you spend the night dreaming of escape, Desmos?" he asked, smiling grimly. Desmos' eyes revealed a quiet fury. His fists tightened in their bonds as he strained, exasperated and impotent.

Betos held up his right hand. "You see this? A man's weapon hand is law here, not the pronouncements of dandified judges and lawyers. Now look—" He held up his mutilated left hand as well. "That happened when I first arrived on the Isle. I had to prove myself in battle, you see. The man who fought me is dead."

Desmos continued to meet his gaze.

"But that's not all *you're* going to lose, my brother. I've spoken to Urdus. You're mine."

Desmos swallowed with difficulty.

"I don't know what he'll do with the rest of the prisoners, once we've gotten away from here but I promise you that you're mine. And on our mother's grave, I promise that you'll pay for every stinking day and night I've spent in the company of these butchers and thugs. Do you understand?"

Desmos looked away.

"Do you understand, brother?"

Droplets of spittle pelted Desmos' face. Desmos blinked them away, then answered in a grave, level voice, "I understand, brother."

Urdus noticed that Athu was absent. "Where is the sorcerer?" he asked Aleil.

"I don't know." Her voice was small; she seemed to shrink away from Urdus.

"Find him," Urdus told her.

"Find him?" Wonder and fear lit her eyes. "I don't know where he is! Leave me alone, Urdus!"

His hand jumped out and gripped her arm. For a moment, Aleil wilted inside. Gods! would this end? Why was she trapped in the middle? What had she done to herself?

At that moment Athu reentered the campsite to see Urdus holding Aleil in a menacing grip.

Athu returned without his cedarwood box.

Urdus let go of the woman. "Where have you been?"

Athu's eyes gleamed brightly. "Walking. What concern is it of yours?"

Urdus' upper lip lifted in a cold sneer, but instead of replying he turned and walked away, shaking his head in feigned contempt. The wizard disturbed him more than he liked to admit.

"Move out!" he yelled to his renegades.

Betos approached. He drew Urdus aside for a moment and whispered in his ear.

"Urdus, do you fear that Shemite?"

But the giant Vanir only growled for answer and turned roughly away.

Aleil came up to Athu, rubbing her upper arms. "Where did you go?" she asked him in an undertone.

Athu's eyes played upon her. "My clay-work," he said.

"Clay-work?" Aleil repeated without comprehension. "What clay-work? Why won't you protect me from Urdus? I'll give you everything—why won't you help me?"

Athu's eyes glowed weirdly.

"Write it," Urdus said to Betos. "Can you fashion a twig well enough to write it?"

Betos nodded and smiled grimly. "Pick a man, Urdus."

Urdus walked to the captives. Sonja, alone, was held in her chains by two men some distance away. Urdus' eyes shifted to Desmos and Hubarthis, then settled sternly upon a young officer whose face was scarred from the battle: half his beard torn away, one eye black-and-blue, a great number of welts showed on his naked chest and limbs.

"You," Urdus said. Then, to three of his men, "Take him out of the bunch."

The young man's eyes lit with fear. His bonds were removed and he was dragged to a tree.

"Nail him up," Urdus commanded. "Use Aquilonian knives."

The young officer's eyes went wide. He writhed frantically, but a cord was tightened around his middle and he was held to the tree. Two burly convicts held his hands together above his head, backs against the rough bark. Then a third shoved a knife through the palms, deep into the wood. The soldier screamed. Two more knives were driven through his feet, so that he hung nailed to the tree with his own comrades' weapons.

His sobs and screams carried from him, rising higher and higher.

Sonja and the other hostages called out for an end, for a quick death to stop the young man's suffering.

"Cut his throat!"

"By Mitra! End the torture, you cowards!"

Betos hastily scrawled a message on a scrap of leather, using a sharpened twig for a pen and the crucified soldier's rilling blood for ink. He then handed it to Urdus, who squinted and scowled at the writing:

Nem estes optiveo Aquiloni. Hubartho ost

*Desmo ebta elemum. Obu orloriem se elemum
kestros elu eldo.*

"Here—I'll read it," said Betos. "It says:

'We have Aquilonian captives. Hubarthis
and Desmos are among them. Do not follow
or they will die like this.' "

Urdus grunted in approval, placed the note against
the young officer's chest, then pinned it there with a
long, thick splinter of wood.

Finally, to the dwindling moans of the dying man, the
captives were herded into the center of the band, and
Urdus and his renegades began their trek farther up the
hillside.

"Why don't we just run away?" Aleil whispered to
Athu.

They were walking a short distance behind the others,
keeping to themselves. Aleil felt frantic to escape; also,
she could not understand why Athu, with his sorcery,
sometimes helped Urdus and the others but usually left
them to fend for themselves as best they might.

"I have a debt to repay," Athu told her.

"What debt? Against Urdus? You want to kill him?"

Athu looked at her.

"Then slay him and be done with it! Let's leave,
Athu!"

"Child," he reprimanded her quietly, musingly. "So
like children, all of you—violent, obscene children."

"But—"

"There is more to it than simply slaying Urdus, Aleil.
I need these people. They shall be an aid to me."

Aleil tossed her dark hair, piqued. "What do you need
them for?"

"For my clay-work. I need their strength, their blood,
their spirits."

Aleil shook her head. Her voice was brittle as she said:

"I thought you would help me—I thought we would help each other get away. I have nothing to do with your —your clay-work."

Athu shrugged. "We are travelling the road of Hell," he told her. "You cannot escape it, no more than I. If you ran from here, you would still be upon the road of Hell. Urdus believes he is leading these fools to freedom, but he is leading them only into the jaws of my trap."

"What *is* your clay-work? What are you doing?"

"You will learn. You will see."

The renegades stopped briefly to lunch on fruit they had found in the thinning forest, to drink water from a trickling stream. Then, moving on, they came upon a clearing and saw a narrow waterfall which poured over a cliffside and fell into a wide pool.

"*Yaaiii!* What devil's work—!"

"Swordskull! It's Swordskull, by Mitra!"

The exclamations had burst from the men in the lead. Urdus cursed and hurried forward, then gasped—for the waterfall spilled from a high, narrow cleft resembling a sword-gash, and the face of the cliff bore an obvious, horrific resemblance to a gigantic, weathered skull.

"Gods of Vanaheim!" roared Urdus, a note of panic mingling with the rage in his voice. "We're not on the mainland—*we're back on Os Harku!*"

"Sorcery!" muttered Otos, his rat-face quivering. "Those river-winds last night—we made no progress. That's why the Aquilonian ship caught up with us so quickly—"

"Aye—*sorcery!*" screamed Urdus, whirling and drawing his great sword.

Aleil was terrified to realize that the giant was coming straight for her. She turned, hoping to appeal to Athu for help—only to find that he was no longer there.

"You witch!" growled Urdus, trembling as he strove to hold his fury in check. "Where is he? Tell me—or I swear I'll rip you into pieces!"

"I—I know not," gasped Aleil, sinking to her knees.

Her voice cracked with fear. "He—was here but a moment ago—"

Urdus and all his men looked about them, but Athu was nowhere to be seen. The surrounding forest was dim and silent. Unconsciously the men moved closer. The sound of the waterfall seemed unnaturally loud.

"He's gone," muttered Betos. "Urdus—we can't stay here."

The Vanir sheathed his sword, turned and faced his lieutenant, glowering. "Aye, Betos, we'll need a new plan now—*damn him!* If this *was* his doing, then I swear by Ymir that I'll—!"

"We've no time for that now, Urdus."

"Aye." The giant glanced up the cliff, then pointed. "There's a ravine just to the left of the skull-face—it will lead us to the top of the cliff where there's a good vantage point. From there, we should be able to see whether there are any more Aquilonian ships offshore."

Betos jerked his head toward the captives. "What about them?"

"Bring them," snarled Urdus. "Guard them more closely than ever. They may now be our *only* chance for freedom."

They climbed the narrow ravine, using its craggy sides and boulder-clogged floor for handholds, roughly hauling up the hostages with ropes. The nearby rushing and crashing of the waterfall half deafened them, and the tumbling waters made the rocks slick with a thin mist of spray so that they had to make their way slowly and carefully to the height.

At the top, the table of the escarpment was wide and flat, stretching to the northeast and sloping gently to a low valley filled with forest and vegetation. Beyond it, Urdus knew, lay Central Lake and the fierce clan of Shihur, the Demoness.

Urdus cursed.

When he looked back towards the river, he could

make out wide patches of it beyond the tops of the trees. He could just see the masts and destroyed sails of the Aquilonian galley.

He could see the whole island from here: the carpet of the treetops and the wide, sprawling, face of the hillside as it made its way down to the fringe of cliffs and forest at the river bank.

Urdus waited as patiently as he could as the remainder of his party slowly ascended the ravine. He had told several of his men to scatter wide during the day's journey; he had thought it very possible that Aquilonian border patrols would be nearby, and thus any far-ranging scouts could catch sight of them and warn Urdus of any surprise maneuver. But then, he had assumed they were on the mainland. Things were different now. If the Aquilonians had spotted the beached ship . . .

The afternoon dwindled, and as the captives were watched in the center of the plateau's wide floor, the first of Urdus' scouts returned with their reports. They had seen no Aquilonian troops, no signs of search parties.

Urdus cast a clouded, calculating eye towards Captain Hubarthis.

Two other scouts remained in the forest. Urdus had sent them together. The afternoon was advancing toward evening, and Urdus fretted at their tardiness. He stared towards the north; from the edge of the stream bank far to the northeast there showed nothing but forest—although, Urdus knew, beyond that forest were the squalid huts and gardens of the criminal clans.

Anger grew in his stomach, knotting and working there, as he let his memory play back upon his hope of escaping to the cities of Aquilonia.

Urdus looked back at his crowd of renegades, not surprised to see many of them grumbling and quarreling. They sat or squatted, eating or drinking, eyes focussed on the captives, especially on Lord Desmos. It had not been Desmos who had damned Urdus to the Isle—but Desmos had condemned some of Urdus' tribe, and the giant knew that with the recent disaster and disappointment, with the fatigue and worry intensifying their hatred, his men were growing eager to get their own kind of justice from Lord Sir Desmos.

A scream, high-pitched, from the forest to the north—

Urdus watched tensely, trying to decide where the scream had come from. Another followed as the first trailed out. Urdus' men hurried to gather around him, staring down at the forest to the north, though they could see nothing.

"Wait," Urdus ordered them in a grim voice. "Keep an eye on the captives."

They waited.

The sun began to sink, quickly, setting miasmal fire to the tops of the pines, oaks and maples that carpeted the land. . . .

Then, as the last of the sun vanished, there was the sound of scruffling movement from the ravine.

One of the scouts, Ulum, staggered toward the camp. The man was torn and bleeding, but he still had his sword. Urdus climbed part-way down and helped his scout up onto the plateau. There Ulum was given water and food. Urdus let him eat and drink before questioning him.

"You found a patrol?"

Ulum shook his head. "We found the advance of a patrol—three Aquilonians. We saw them before they spotted us, so we waited for them—struck down the first two quickly enough, but the third gave us trouble. He wounded me—" Ulum indicated the gash upon his forearm "—and slew Taris. But I downed him at last."

"We heard the screams," said Betos. "Yet, we saw no new Aquilonian ship—"

"Doubtless it was hidden by the trees near the shore," Otos grunted.

"They'll track us down!" said another man.

"We're safe here," cautioned Urdus, his natural leadership overcoming his anger. "We have enough men to defend this roost. But since we know they're coming, no fires. And twice the guard of last night. Understood?"

They all assented.

Night fell. The convicts prepared for sleep. Urdus advised Betos to sleep near Otos. Betos agreed to sleep with his knife out, and passed the word to the guards to be watchful.

The captives were set into the center of the camp. They whispered together as the renegades fell to sleep.

"My bonds may be loosening," Desmos said.

Hubarthis shook his head. "It's your imagination, my friend. We're bound with chains as well as rope."

"Rope can be worked loose," Sonja said.

"But the chains?" said another Aquilonian.

"We've all tested the links," Hubarthis sighed.

"They've cut the links often enough," Sonja reminded them. "The iron is soft. If we could get a steel blade—"

"But how many of us would that free?" Desmos asked.

"One," said Sonja, "would be enough."

Footsteps behind them—Urdus.

"Quiet!" he said grimly. "You can't break those chains."

"Yet, we'll be free in any case," said Hubarthis sternly, "and that soon. We all heard your men jabbering. So you thought you were on the mainland, eh? And now, here you are back on Os Harku!" The officer laughed. "You hoped to use us to bargain for your freedom, if need be—well, now it looks like you'll need to bargain for your lives, and feel fortunate if we're worth the price."

Urdus stood tall, scowling, like a judging Vanir god. "I swear to you, Aquilonian, that if we do not gain our freedom by this exploit, you will surely die with us!"

Hubarthis seemed somewhat taken aback; but Desmos, to Sonja's surprise, suddenly leaned forward as much as his bonds would allow and said, "But, think, man! Is there no other way open to you?"

"Ha!" Urdus chuckled somberly. "You judged us—and now you fear death at the hand of the brother you condemned. Well, I don't blame you for your fear, for if I judge Betos' anger aright your death is likely to be extremely slow. Still, I'd protect you from him if I thought your hide was worth anything—"

"Listen, Urdus," said Desmos, "your only chance is to get off this island in the galley you beached—preferably before dawn. If an Aquilonian warship hasn't spotted it by now, it soon will. You know I speak the truth."

Sonja wondered what stratagem Desmos was plotting, decided he was trying to buy them time—and her estimation of him went up a notch. But Hubarthis cried, "Desmos, you traitor!"

Urdus laughed.

"Fear not, Hubarthis—this coward can make no bargains with me. I had already decided upon the very thing he has suggested. Tomorrow we destroy your Aquilonian friends. If we succeed, Hubarthis, I may let you live —for you are a brave man, even as I am, and I admire you for it. But as for this Desmos, who has condemned so many of us to this Isle in the name of his brand of justice—well, he shall soon learn from his brother the nature of justice in the real world. And—" he cast his dark, vindictive eyes upon Sonja—"as for this lip-biting harridan, she also shall experience some hard facts."

"By Tarim," Sonja swore, not able to look behind her to see Urdus because of her chains, "either free us or kill us! Do not game with us this way!"

Urdus turned on his heel and walked off.

Sonja and Hubarthis continued to pull at their chains, frustrated but working, working to free themselves.

Major Thobis and his squad stood staring regretfully at the three Aquilonian corpses and the renegade body a little farther on. Thobis looked up and seemed to sniff the air.

"I was right," he said. "The criminals who took Commander Hubarthis' galley are near."

"How can we know, sir?" said a soldier. "True, we saw the ship where it lay aground south of here, but such often put ashore to leave criminals—"

Thobis shook his head. "It was running a distress pennant. We'll rest for an hour. Break out your rations. You six men, bury those bodies."

"And the renegade?"

"Leave him to rot."

While they ate, Thobis sat in silence, thinking. He blamed himself, somewhat, for the deaths. Perhaps he should have ordered the whole company ahead at once.

It was a strange business, this pursuit of the escapees from Os Harku. Thobis knew that two galleys had been dispatched downriver in pursuit; he and his troops had gone in the ship that had skirted the east side of the island. All night they had fought a perverse wind; evidently that wind had been combined with a strange upstream current, also—for when the dawn came they had found themselves just to the north of the prison-isle. And far away to the southwest they had barely caught sight of their sister-ship, the one under command of Commander Hubarthis. Shortly after, they had plied toward it and observed that it seemed to be engaged with another ship; but they could not be sure, for both ships were gone shortly—vanished in the direction of the western shore of Os Harku.

It was over three hours later that, cruising along the west shore, Thobis and his men spotted the beached ship with the pennant of distress fluttering from its highest mast. A skiff was hurriedly dispatched, but no life was found aboard.

"There may be survivors," Thobis had suggested. "A large party appears to have gone inland. They may have hostages."

"What will you do?" asked the commander of the galley.

Thobis scowled. "This southwestern portion of the Isle is said to be shunned by the exiles for superstitious reasons." He turned and faced the captain squarely. "Set me and my troops ashore just north of here—say half a league. It may be we'll catch them as they try to flee the region."

But it had not turned out that way, and now Major Thobis sat in the silent forest with his squad as they ate their rations, wondering what his next move would be.

Urdus stood watch. In the middle of the night, he saw Athu ascend the ravine and enter the encampment. The Vanir's sharp, angry whisper brought the Shemite about.

Athu waited while Urdus approached him. "Where do you think you're going?" asked the Vanir in a low, heavy voice.

"What concern is it of yours, Urdus?"

Urdus bristled. "Don't question me, traitor. I think you're going to answer a few questions."

"You do not give me orders."

"Shemite cur!" Urdus drew back his hand to strike Athu, but the look in the wizard's eyes suddenly made him change his mind. Those eyes gleamed cold, luminous. He lowered his hand. "No one leaves the group," he went on in a softer tone. "Where did you go today?"

"To do my clay-work. I'm going to kill you, Urdus. Do you realize that? Just as I brought you back to Os Harku. I caused it, and I am going to slay you. Surely you sense that. Why else do you think I am tagging along on this parade of yours? You're going to the Hells, Urdus—and I'm leading you there, right by the nose."

Urdus growled and lifted his hand again.

Athu barked softly, like a Stygian jackal, and moved; his hand darted out silently with the speed of a cobra, and his fingers touched Urdus' neck between the collarbone and the veins of his throat.

Urdus was frozen. He could not move; sharp, darting

series of sparks seemed to shoot down his body, paralyzing him. He stared at the stocky Shemite. Sweat broke out on him.

Athu laughed softly. "I advise you to harm Aleil no more," he told Urdus. "Henceforth she is mine, and therefore outside the disgusting animal world you rule."

Urdus tried to sneer, to spit, even to cough.

"The effect will wear off shortly," Athu continued. "But remember this: I am going to kill you. I could have killed you now, but I have my reasons for waiting. I would have you feel fear—and you shall. You will know who I am and what I am—for I am no longer an ordinary wizard, but the servant of monstrous gods."

With that he turned and left, walking away into the darkness.

Urdus stared after him, watching him go—frightened that he was so powerless, that he could be thus reduced to a statue by the merest touch from that damned Shemite's fingers. . . .

When Athu was well away from the campsite, far down the cliffside, he stopped walking and spent a moment in deep concentration—then let himself float into the air. For some distance he hovered above the ground, then spread his robed arms, lifted higher and began to float on the slow wind currents.

He could not travel for a long distance in this way, for his energy was not limitless—but it would serve to get him to the riverbank in a much shorter time than would walking . . .

He was dimly aware that he passed by living things in the forest as he drifted on, for he was deep in the sort of concentration that made him aware of the world's immediacy. Small nightbirds flitted before him, lit and then unlit by alternating shafts of bright moonlight and desolate shadows that hung in the deeper recesses of the forest. The trees became denser. The ground sloped down, and Athu followed its descent.

At last he became more conscious and lowered himself to his feet. Parting shrubbery and passing through foliage, he came to the bank of the Shirki. A short distance below him, to the south, stood the wrecked Aquilonian galley. Far out in the middle of the river another ship floated by: obviously an aristocratic barge, for it was lit with hundreds of lights. Athu sneered—but then, for an instant, felt almost a pity for those who knew nought of reality . . .

Stepping into the river, he waded out a short distance, then rolled up his right sleeve and thrust his arm into the water to the elbow.

He felt the emanations from the pleasure barge, wild and obvious and bold. But he also sensed something farther up, to the north—another ship, perhaps a day distant. A heavy ship, armed. He could sense it in the water.

A ship that had put ashore Aquilonian troops, perhaps?

Athu sighed and sipped of the water, then returned to the bank. Once more he lifted his arms to the air; his feet left the earth, and he floated inland again, returning to the spot where he had worked the previous night.

Aleil was roused from an uncertain sleep by a premonition. She was lying just outside the perimeter of the campsite. Perhaps it was the tread of one of Urdus' guards which awoke her, though when she sat up she saw that the nearest guards were some distance away, talking amongst themselves.

She sat up and stretched, looking around. Yes; she sensed something—perhaps something her witch instincts had told her. She rose up and, ignored by the guards, began to walk towards the lip of the plateau.

There was a figure standing there in the darkness. It took no great effort to determine that the massive back and shoulders belonged to Urdus. Aleil crept up to him. Urdus groaned, and Aleil saw him lower his right arm slowly, as if with difficulty.

She made noise as she approached, but Urdus did not respond. Aleil was puzzled. She came around and cautiously faced him.

Urdus fixed her with a wild stare.

"What's the matter with you?" she asked him.

Urdus apparently could not answer her. He groaned, and tried to move his arm again.

Insight struck her. "Gods!" she breathed. "What has Athu done to you?"

Urdus' face twitched, as if he were trying to communicate his rage and anguish.

Aleil tittered, then began to laugh. She sensed Urdus becoming more and more enraged. Half-fearful, she covered her mouth with her hands, but still she coughed silently, absolutely unsuccessful in hiding her perverse amusement at Urdus' predicament.

"Athu, wasn't it?" she asked him, abandoning all attempt to hide her mirth. "Oh, you fool! You think you can do anything with anyone. You fool! Has Athu put a curse on you?"

Her laughter died and she smirked, then scowled at Urdus. She put her hands on her hips and sauntered back and forth, parading before the Vanir and mocking him.

"Shall I bite your lip off, Urdus?" she whispered to him tensely. "Heh? Shall I finish the job your red-haired prisoner began? Or, perhaps I'll pin a note to your flesh! Heh? Would you like that? Or even better, perhaps I'll grab hold of your hair and *throw you* down with one hand! Would you like that? Heh? The great Urdus, thrown down by a woman's hand?"

Urdus' frustration and anger showed in his face, but he could do naught.

"No . . ." Aleil went on. "No. Perhaps I'll simply summon a serpent from the woods. Would you like that, Urdus? I'll have him bite you sixty times, all over your legs and feet, and you won't be able to move at all, will you? It'll bite you again and again, and you won't be able to do anything to stop it."

Urdus was sweating.

"Perhaps I'll have an owl swoop down and peck your eyes out. Heh, Urdus? Would you like that? Heh?"

He tried to move his arm again, but the feeling inside his numbness grew but gradually, and he could not coax it.

"Perhaps," Aleil said, in a voice more softened, "perhaps I'll just leave you here and you can wonder about all the things Athu and I *could* do to you if we wanted to. Heh?"

She stared into Urdus' eyes, sneered, then turned and left. Urdus heard her walking away, listened as her footsteps vanished into the silence of the nighted camp. He tried to look behind, but could not.

He waited. Pain would sparkle somewhere inside him, and a bit more feeling would return—slowly, agonizingly. His arm dropped a bit lower.

And then a serpent appeared.

Urdus saw it in a patch of moonlight. Terrified, he tried to move but could not.

Aleil, he thought. *She truly is a witch!*

The serpent came close, its fat body looping sidewise on the rocky ground, glimmering slightly in the moonlight, its tongue flickering and flickering from its large, heart-shaped head, smelling him out.

Urdus watched it until it disappeared from his view, somewhere under his bearded cheeks.

He felt it slithering slowly over his boots.

Had he still retained feeling, he would have lost control of his bowels in that moment of fright.

But nothing more happened. Urdus waited—and waited—until at last he began to hope the snake had gone. Mentally, he relaxed a bit. Yes, the serpent must be gone. . . .

Then there came a noise, behind him.

Men's bootsteps—his guards.

"By Mitra! Is that Urdus?"

"Why doesn't he move?"

"Urdus, what's wrong with you?"

"Gods! He seems paralyzed! Here—here—take him! Lay him down!"

Urdus tried to scream: *No! No! Don't lay me down, the serpent may be there!*

But it was not there, and the guards laid Urdus down and kept watch over him as his feelings gradually returned.

"How could this have happened?" one asked.

"That Shemite!" exclaimed another.

"Aye, surely that sorcerer! Athu!"

"Cursed be his seed, it was Athu!"

Their commotion woke up the camp. Sonja awoke, aching from her long confinement. She shook her head and leaned forward.

Whatever the problem was, she regretted immensely that her bonds were not loosened enough for her to take advantage of it, to enable her to grab one of the Aquilonian weapons that lay in the rolled blanket by the edge of the campsite. She knew her sword was there, with the other confiscated weapons.

Throne of Erlik! Why had she not fought more desperately against the sorcerous power that had made her give up her sword?

Through the night Athu worked, gathering up soft clay and earth in his animal-skin robe. He worked naked, his dark skin and smooth movements betraying him no more than the shadows or the whispering wind betrayed any other living things in the forest.

When he had gathered enough clay and soil in his robe, he took it and his wooden box up to the small cave which formed the left socket of the face of Swordskull.

Several more times during the night Athu went into the cave, returned for clay and soil, returned again to the cave. A short while before dawn, when he decided he had accomplished enough, he bathed in the pool and

dressed himself, then set a secret invisible sign upon the
opening of the cave, barring it from intrusion. This accomplished, he returned, floating on the low, drifting
mists, up towards Urdus' encampment.

Just after dawn, Sergeant Major Thobis and his men
came upon the old campsite—and the cold firepits, the
bits of bones and fruit pulp, and the corpse of the
crucified officer.

Thobis read the note pinned to the young officer's
chest. He cursed.

One of his corporals looked east, towards the cliffs.

"Yes," Thobis said, nodding. "Of course. That's
where they would head."

"Shall we wait for reinforcements, Sergeant? There
may yet be some arriving from the other galley."

"And there may not. We're not even sure if Lobor's
galley has decided to return this way yet. We can't send
up smoke—that would betray our position."

"At least we know that Hubarthis is alive."

Thobis shook his head. "We know he was alive, maybe, at the time this note was written." He turned to his
men. "Break your fast, now. Rest. Then, we'll assail this
cliff. Have you a map, corporal?"

The soldier produced a crumpled piece of parchment
from his belt and displayed it.

Thobis traced the lineaments upon it with a finger
whose nail had been bit to the quick. "We'll go around,"
he said at last. "It would be too dangerous for us to
attack from this side. They'd expect it. We'll go around,
through the forest, and come up the other side, where it
isn't so steep and where the forest will hide us."

The corporal nodded. Thobis refolded the map and
handed it back to him. "We'll go around. . . ."

Chapter 7

The decision was made.

Urdus and his men stood up. Betos was there, and three dozen others. Otos was not among them, nor a handful of stalwarts who were sympathetic with him.

They crossed the camp in a rank, Urdus and his men, eyes upon the sorcerer.

Athu was resting upon the ground, his head pillowed against the roots of a tall tree, as he had been since dawn. His eyes were half shut. Aleil was beside him.

When the band of criminals had come within a dozen paces of Athu, Urdus grunted and held up a hand. Urdus growled, "Stand up."

Athu opened his eyes wide, like the undead at nightfall. Aleil, alarmed, stared at Urdus questioningly, but he did not so much as look at her.

"I told you to stand up."

Athu did so, slowly, taking his time. Urdus temper rose. When the Shemite was on his feet, Urdus told him:

"Get out."

Athu smiled darkly.

"Go," Urdus repeated.

The many bearded, sun-darkened faces behind him scowled silently upon the Shemite.

"Go?" said Athu. "Leave the encampment?"

"Get away from here. You are no longer human. Stay away from us."

Athu stared at him for a moment, then threw back his head and barked a laugh. "Fools!" he exclaimed. "Do you think you can rid yourselves of me of your own will?"

Aleil was frightened. Sonja and the other prisoners, bound in the wide center of the campsite, stared curiously. Otos and his handful, standing farther off, wondered what this portended for them.

Urdus took a step forward. "*Begone*, magician! We do not want you near us, contaminating us with your poisonous sorcery!"

Athu shook his head soberly. "I go nowhere, Urdus, until and unless I decide to do so myself. But your request was to be expected. There are certain conditions, however, which must first be met."

Urdus growled. His men pushed forward.

"I want one of the prisoners."

The Vanir shook his head.

"I want the red-haired woman."

"You get nothing, blood-sucker!" Urdus told him. "You may be a sorcerer, but you cannot fight all of us. Be glad I'm letting you walk away."

"I will haunt you, Urdus."

"Get out!"

"I will return, Urdus. I will not stray far. I have marked you. You will not escape me."

"You don't frighten me!" Urdus drew his sword slowly, deliberately. "If you try to touch me again, I'll hack your head off. And these men'll quarter you, and drive a stake through your heart."

Athu sneered. "I could destroy you all with a gesture."

"I don't believe that," said Urdus. "You're part magician and part charlatan. Maybe you've sold your soul to some devil, but you can die by steel, and your strength can't last forever."

"Then why not slay me now?" said the Shemite evenly.

"I'm giving you a chance to leave, Athu. Take it." Urdus' sword trembled in his grip—eager, losing patience.

Athu shrugged. "I want the red-haired woman. Her spirit is strong. I can use her."

"No. Take Aleil. Use her."

Aleil moved closer to Athu.

Athu stared at the Vanir for a long moment. "Then I tell you this," he said, "Your days are numbered on the road of Hell, Urdus—yours and all your men's. I will not stray far; I will watch. I will kill you, Urdus—I, and none other. Do you understand that?"

"Go!"

"Do you understand?"

"*Begone!*" Urdus heaved forward, lifting his sword.

Athu did not move. Urdus paused. The Shemite motioned to Aleil to get behind him, to start down the ravine; then, with a last dark look to Urdus and his band, he turned his back on them and followed Aleil.

Urdus stepped back a pace; he half-turned and nodded to Betos.

Betos slapped the shoulder of a man next to him. The man was armed with a bow, and had an arrow already nocked to its string.

Athu's skin-cloaked back was vanishing among some small trees near the cliff edge; bright golden and green leaves fluttered past him. He began to step down the side of the cliff.

The archer moved forward, lifted his bow, took aim, and released his arrow with a heavy twang.

Sonja started. Desmos swore. Hubarthis paused in his efforts to work free of his chains.

The feathered arrow struck Athu between his shoulder blades. He slumped and dropped out of sight. Aleil screamed from below the lip of the cliff.

Urdus grunted with satisfaction. His eyes were wide, his arms flexed; spittle drooled from his lips into his beard. Otos, standing on the other side of the encampment with his men, whispered frantically, "He's mad! They're going to murder us all!"

Aleil's scream died out. There was a crashing noise from beyond the trees on the edge of the precipice. Urdus took a step forward. Then a sudden howl of anguish rose up—Athu's—and a clambering sound, a scruffling on rocks, the snapping of branches.

Urdus paled. Sweat broke out on his forehead and neck.

Aleil screamed anew.

Otos stood breathless, watching. And Urdus and his men watched, too, silent and grim, as first one hand and then another—white, veined, bloody hands—reached over the edge of the precipice and grappled with roots and moss, pulling forward. Arms clad in leathern sleeves —then the dark hair, matted and dirty with bits of twigs and leaves, and the eyes—the horrible eyes, yellow and on fire—

"Ymir!" Urdus swore, his voice cracking.

Athu pulled himself up over the edge, tumbled to his knees, stretched out his arms and howled. Slobber drooled down his beard. His eyes sparked.

"Fools!" he shrieked. Awkwardly he reached behind him, groped blindly and wrapped his fingers around the shaft of the arrow that protruded from him.

Urdus' men fell back, horrified. The archer dropped his bow and stepped back, uncertain whether to remain and stare or run for his life away from the sorcerer.

Athu, shrieking some insane words in a language which no one comprehended, held up the long shaft in one bloody hand. Aleil showed her frightened face from beyond the edge.

Athu threw the arrow. "Hya uatha na huytber!" he screamed.

The archer turned and ran. Urdus' men howled—for as soon as the arrow left Athu's fingers, it transformed into a flying serpent: the bloody arrow point became fanged jaws, the shaft a sleek, scaly body, the feathering expanded into wings.

The archer stumbled, looked back, lifted his arms instinctively over his head for protection. He screamed to see the serpent squirming through the air at him on its feathery wings. He tried to scramble back to his feet.

Athu reeled. Aleil ran up and held onto him.

But all eyes were on the archer who, regaining his feet, tried to run backwards from the serpent, flailing his arms and screaming. He stumbled again, over the rocks of a fire pit, and slammed down on his back.

The flying serpent dove straight at him.

The archer shrieked and kicked, foam flying from his lips. Frantically he caught up a rock, flung it futilely—

And the serpent struck him full in the chest.

The man howled in agony, writhing, as the thing transformed once again into a feathered arrow, piercing him through the heart. Then he collapsed upon the rocks and lay still.

Silence.

Urdus breathed. His men began to whisper.

Betos ran toward the cliff. Athu and Aleil were already gone. A trail of blood led down over the precipice edge, disappeared into the tangled verdure of the ravine.

"They're gone!" Betos called back to Urdus.

"Let them go!" Urdus went to the archer, who lay frozen in death on the rocky ground. "Let them go," he whispered coldly to himself. "Ymir . . . !"

Major Thobis was not by nature a brave man. He was an ordinary man with an ordinary spirit, and instead of spending his days searching through forests for escaped criminals, he would far rather have remained in Tanasul with his wife and her mother and his children, eking out a borderline income as a scribe in some office of the local bureaucracy. His goal in life was to retire to his small country estate, there to remain a gentleman farmer —Thobis loved a good garden. But a well-meaning friend had gained him a military post that paid better than clerking, and a few seasons of life's vicissitudes had led him to this uncomfortable garrison outpost on a wild stretch of the Shirki, leagues from civilization and from his wife and family.

At night, before retiring, he had considered those vicissitudes.

While he believed in the gods, Thobis—not an unintelligent man, though perhaps a not very assertive one—reasoned that the tides and fortunes of life are more often determined by totally mundane circumstances and motivations. His friend, Arus, for instance—a handsome man, one who wore his armor well . . . Thobis had seen his wife's gaze linger several times upon Arus' trim military figure when she thought Thobis had not noticed.

Vicissitudes, indeed.

So here he was, in the middle of a wild forest on an island of the damned, leading a squadron of privates and mercenaries against a troop of convicts led by some sort of savage barbarian. In what better fashion, Thobis reflected, could he show his selfless love for his wife than by dying heroically against an outlaw band, and leaving her guiltless in the arms of Arus?

He decided that he was neither selfless nor heroic, and that he did not care to die at the hands of these felons.

He and his men were on the eastern side of the forested escarpment, well-hidden from elevated view by the thick tangle of trees and undergrowth. Thobis consulted first the sun—it was past mid-morning, he realized—and then the rude map of Os Harku which the government in its bureaucratic genius had supplied the garrison: map at least a decade out of date. Thobis remembered consulting maps in Tanasul which clearly marked the island far better than the crude sketch now in his hands. Staring at the map, and wiping at the mosquitoes and flies buzzing around him, he searched his memory for clues and details cursorily noticed years earlier.

Finally, deliberately, he rolled up the map. No clues.

"Straight up, now," he said to Corporal Nothos. "We can scale this escarpment before midafternoon. If our criminals aren't up there, at least we'll have a better vantage point to guess their direction.''

"All right, sir.''

The corporal made a sign, and the men of the squadron hefted their armor for the assault on the cliff.

"And tell the boys,'' Thobis sighed, ''not to make too much noise. Understood?''

Corporal Nothos nodded and pivoted about, cupped his hands to his mouth and bellowed, "As quietly as Picts, now! No undue noise to alert these dogs to our approach!''

His voice rang and echoed and died out somewhere in the fastness of the forest. A few men grinned ironically.

Thobis sighed again and shook his head, whispered a blasphemous prayer to Mitra, and led the way up the escarpment.

The strain was beginning to show upon Otos and his comrades.

Urdus and his three dozen men kept their silence and their distance. They were all in a conference around Urdus' cold campfire, whispering and glancing occasionally at Otos and his handful, keeping a watchful eye upon the captives.

"They intend to kill us all,'' one of Otos' men said grimly in an undertone. "They're afraid the Aquilonians are going to close in and they can't afford to trust us.''

Desmos strained against his bonds, but they had not given before and they did not give now. He sighed heavily and said to Sonja, "They're going to kill us.''

Her stare was fixed murderously, levelled upon Urdus and his band.

"They're not going to kill us,'' she muttered. "I believe they're going to break up their band and move on. They may still need us as hostages if they're going to try to escape in the crippled galley.''

Hubarthis said quietly: "If only one of us could get free. If only one of us—''

"I've got it!" Sonja hissed, and her shoulders strained in betrayal of her efforts behind her back.

All the prisoners held their breath.

"Keep staring at Urdus," Hubarthis commanded them.

Sonja cursed. "Damn it! No . . . ! Mitra damn them! Hubarthis, look at my chain. Can you see it?"

"I don't dare look. They may notice—"

"Can you feel it? Can you?"

He sidled closer to her, strained to reach his captive right hand towards hers. Tips of three fingers plucked at Sonja's sweaty wrists and scraped along the length of chain. "Aye—one link," he breathed.

"They loosened and refastened it," Sonja told him, "when they moved me this morning. Damn! It's so close—!"

"Careful!" Desmos said. "They're getting up. Calm down, now, Sonja."

They watched the renegades. Urdus rose to his feet first, hand on sword, towering above the men seated around him. He was looking at Otos and his band. The giant nodded and waved his hand at Otos.

Otos studied the faces of his men, then rose and took a few steps towards Urdus.

"Come forward," demanded the Vanir.

"I do not trust you!" Otos called to him.

"We want to talk to you."

"Then speak from where you stand!"

Urdus shrugged. "All right. You're free to leave. Go your own way, you and your men."

"You will slay us treacherously if we try to leave!"

"No!" Urdus shook his head contemptuously. "No. You helped us to fight free, so you may live. Your anger against me means nothing, but without your loyalty I cannot trust you when it comes to fighting the Aquilonians. Go."

Otos seemed to waver a moment. He waited, thinking Then: "We want four of the captives."

Urdus scowled; he turned back to his men. Most of them shook their heads, spitting or sneering with contempt. Urdus looked back to Otos.

"No."

Otos scowled in anger. "No prisoners? But the Aquilonians will slay us if they find us—"

"So?"

"But—we need them for ransom . . ." Otos began.

"They will not be ransom for *you*," Urdus told him calmly.

"Give us just one, then—the Hyrkanian woman—"

Urdus shook his head.

"Now, go," he told Otos. "You and your men—get out."

It is difficult to break the forced habits of years. Athu, before his banishment to the Isle, had become atrophied in his response to humans—had become worse than alienated. Years of probing into the borderlands beyond the physical world had taken their toll. A woman's light touch seemed to him almost a premeditated attack—an assault.

But in the harsh social environment of Os Harku, Athu had found some of his humanity being roughly reawakened—his anger, his fear, and his desire for a woman. And he hated it.

On the borderland of the occult world, human emotions dissolve into wider worlds of cosmic significance. The human soul seems a fragment of driftwood caught in slow ocean tides of time, thrown upon deadly cold beaches that extend infinitely across a wonderland, a terrorland far more intense and vast than any warm, fleshy world.

How could he explain this to Aleil?

Why should he explain this to Aleil?

Her crude perceptions, her human sense of meaning and her selfish, fearful manipulations meant nothing to him. She did not want to be harmed, so she clung to him, and thus did not want him harmed. Dependency of any sort works cruelly—but who is at fault?

For was not Athu himself dependent upon his hatred for Urdus? Dependent upon his devotion for the clay-work? Dependent on his dark master, Ordru, to whom he had sold his soul for vengeance?

He had estranged himself from the world of man, and in ways far more devastating than any social estrangement suffered by his erstwhile companions of the Isle. . .

While Athu thought thus, Aleil ministered to him. The Shemite lay prone beside the wide pool beneath the escarpment; and there Aleil, following his instructions, had dipped certain broad leaves into the water of the pool and then wiped them upon the magician's wound. She was amazed. Under her fingers the rubbed leaves began to secrete a yellowish liquid, which turned pink when it ran with Athu's blood. Incredibly, the pinkish liquid seemed to work a miracle, to seep as if with a will of its own into the deep arrow-wound. As Aleil rubbed more and more of the wet leaves upon the sorcerer's naked back, she seemed to erase his pain. And finally she seemed to erase even the puncture mark of the arrow, the hole that had been so deep and profusely bleeding.

She paused in wonder, half afraid.

"Do not stop," Athu told her, his lips resting upon one forearm as he lay there, "until the wound is entirely healed."

"But—what is in these leaves that cures an arrow bite?"

"It is not just the leaves. It is myself." After a pause as she continued to rub with the leaves, "I have made supernatural alliance, and the being I serve has endowed me with a vitality unknown to ordinary men."

The comment sent a slight chill through Aleil. "I don't understand," she whispered.

Athu snorted. "Of course not," he said. "You sti

think of yourself in terms of—" He stopped, and lifted his head. "Listen."

Aleil held back with the leaves. "What? I hear nothing." Then, "Mitra! Is it Urdus?"

"Silence." Athu sat up, pushed away Aleil's hand. "Stay here." He rose and left her and hurried into the forest. Within a moment she was alone with her fears—fears not drowned out by the thunder of the waterfall.

Yet, before those fears had time to expand much under the heat of her imagination, Athu had returned.

"What was it?"

"Otos and his men. Apparently they have escaped—or Urdus and his band have set them free."

"Why?"

"For the same reason he cast us out, Aleil. He wishes unity in his ranks. But—I also sense many others in the forest. Aquilonians—"

Screams rang out, cutting the air from high above. They echoed dimly through the trees, carrying distantly and dying out—to be followed by more screams, and still more.

"Mitra!" Aleil gasped, clutching her hands together.

Athu smiled grimly. "The Aquilonians!" he murmured. "They're attacking Urdus and his crew."

"Gods!"

"Come." Athu reached out for her hand.

"You want to go back *there?*"

"I will have those sacrifices. I will have that blood—it is essential to my clay-work. And I will not let Urdus be slain!"

The thin line between Aleil's dependence upon the sorcerer, and her utter fear of him, vanished. Timidly she drew back; but at the sight of the spectral fire in the Shemite's eyes, she just as timidly bent forward and took his rough hand.

"Gods of the gods!" Thobis swore, peering through the last line of trees that protected his soldiers and himself from full view. The renegades—and their hostages!"

"Hubarthis!" Nothos yelled in surprise.

"Damn you!" Thobis hissed at his corporal. "They've heard us. Hurry—ready the men. We must charge!"

Before them, Urdus the giant stood with legs braced as he lifted his sword, wondering at the sound he had just heard. Around him in a loose group stood his men, staring apprehensively toward the forest.

"Rally, you dogs!" roared Urdus suddenly.

And Thobis, drawing his sword as his troops raced up to group behind him, howled the first thing that came to his mind:

"For Aquilonia!"

Urdus' men looked up, staggered—to see what seemed a growing army of Aquilonian troops rushing upon them from the forest on the north side of the plateau.

"At them!" Urdus bellowed.

Sonja jerked forward, straining, as boots and legs raced past her, as howls began to fill the air. She had to get free—now.

The two groups clashed, Thobis and Urdus at the fore, both men running and swinging their blades, the steel meeting with ringing force and an explosion of sparks. Behind Thobis, the forest vomited a line of Aquilonian troops, until Urdus and his men wondered how many damned Aquilonians were hidden there. The renegades met them, swords flashing and clanging, boots kicking, arms and bodies working frantically.

Urdus howled hugely and worked ahead, forcing Thobis back with his great blade. The warring factions scattered more widely; here two men duelled upon the boulders, there two Aquilonians were cutting down a convict as he sought shelter behind a tree. Another of Thobis' soldiers slipped on a root and went down: his head was lopped from his shoulders.

"Dog!" Urdus roared at Thobis. "Call off your men, or we'll kill the captives!"

But Thobis only redoubled his efforts and again

yelled, "For Aquilonia!"

Urdus cursed as he barely avoided a savage thrust at his belly. Roaring with rage, he charged and swung. Thobis' automatic reaction was all that saved him as he interposed his sword between his head and the Vanir's mighty blow; the shock of it numbed his arm, drove his own blade back against his helmet with crashing force and sent him sprawling, half-stunned.

"That's how to kill Aquilonians!" bellowed Urdus to his men. "Cut them down! Kill them all!"

He backed away from the raging battle, backed through the loose ranks of his men, then turned and strode rapidly to where the prisoners lay bound. Sonja saw his eyes glaring madly, his reddish beard flecked with foam.

"I swore an oath!" he howled, brandishing his great blade aloft. "Freedom for us, or death for you—so now, by Ymir's axe, you *die!*"

Urdus' sword came down in a red arc; the head of a black-haired young soldier crunched and sped into the air, struck the ground and rolled against a log, while the blood arced from his neck. His corpse fell lopsided, deluging the man next to him with blood. The other prisoners were fighting ferociously with their bonds, each screaming for a sword, a knife, any weapon to prove himself.

"Coward!" shrieked the man next to the slain one. "Butcher! give me a sword—!"

Next to him sat Hubarthis, his head lifted back, straining his limbs to the utmost in a vain attempt to break his bonds. And next to him—Sonja.

"Dog!" she screamed at Urdus. "Filth! Lice of Erlik!" She strained against her bonds as furiously as Hubarthis—and felt the weak link in her chain give way.

Urdus' sword came down at the screaming soldier next to Hubarthis.

Sonja, struggling furiously, felt the link part entirely. Her bonds went slack.

Urdus' sword struck solidly into the soldier's neck.

Abruptly the man ceased screaming and fell sideways, cloven nearly in two with a diagonal cut through the chest. Blood gushered. Hubarthis cursed furiously.

But Sonja was free. Without pausing she leaped up and ran to the rolled blanket of weapons, grabbed up a sword, pivoted about—and fell to the ground as her half-numbed limbs betrayed her.

Hubarthis yelled: "Sonja! Behind!"

But Sonja, rising to her knees, already saw him: not Urdus, but one of his dogs broken free of the battle and making for her. The renegade paused in mid-stride, or attempted to, when he saw that he faced Sonja's sword point; he unbalanced himself. Sonja lunged from a low crouch, parried his sword and took him through the heart, instantly drew back and skewered him again through the bowels.

The rogue tipped to one side, grinning hideously, eyes wide and full of hate upon her as he dropped to his knees.

Sonja kicked the sword from his fingers. It slid on the ground. As the lout's head struck the earth, Sonja retrieved his blade and ran for the captives, angry and ready for battle.

But battle was already there. The Aquilonians were pushing into the camp, and Urdus and his men were too busy defending themselves to stop her. Howls—screams —the crunch of steel meeting arm, neck, chest—more screams . . . Sonja saw three men go down in a flurry, one of them from Thobis' band.

"Hurry, Sonja!" Hubarthis yelled.

She stooped and sawed quickly through the cord that held him, then frantically began forcing apart links of chain with her sword-point.

"Quickly!" Desmos urged her. "They see us!"

But the criminals were too busy fighting to pay attention to the captives. All the Aquilonians strained at their bonds, while Sonja continued to sever chain-links.

Hubarthis worked free. He jumped up, ran for the bundle of weapons and dragged it over.

A scream close by—one of the renegades had cut down an Aquilonian and now turned to attack Sonja. She made a last cut at the links of Desmos' chain, then turned with her sword up and ready.

Combat, sword-to-sword—red battle! Sonja reveled in it; after nearly two days of prostrate captivity, all the rage that had built up in her, all the madness that had been captive with her now exploded in a whirlwind of swordsmanship and vengeful fury.

The renegade had no chance. Sonja slashed him across the face; steel rang on bone, and the man fell and died before he had even a chance to scream.

Desmos was free. Without pause, without a second thought, he staggered to the bundle of weapons and snatched up a sword. He recognized it as Sonja's and called to her.

"Free the rest of them!" she cried.

He held up the sword; she nodded and threw hers to him, point down, pommel spinning. Desmos threw his at the same time; it was a game he had played during practice sessions as a boy—the way to throw a sword to a companion . . . His instincts came back, reborn in that moment after two days of captivity and anxiety, of living with his exiled brother's taunts and torments.

He caught the sword; Sonja caught hers. She would have moved ahead then against Urdus' men, but Desmos moved first. Sonja let him go.

"*Betos!*" he screamed.

His brother was aiding a fellow ruffian bring down an Aquilonian.

"Betos! *Face me!*"

A crooked smile strained Betos' blood-smeared face as he turned. He waved his sword as if to free it of red droplets, then grinned madly and charged.

Sonja worked anxiously to free the other Aquilonians, with so much of the chain and rope already sundered they were doing it themselves. She handed over swords as the men ran to her. One of them said, "Go on—fight them. I'll free the rest. Go now!"

Sonja nodded, turned, gauged how the battle was going—then saw Urdus engaged again with Thobis, and made for them.

Athu and Aleil crouched on the edge of the precipice, watching. They were well-hidden by the forest, and the fierce battles to the death were scattered widely over the plateau, but nowhere near them.

"Stay back," muttered Athu, "and keep silent."

Aleil was frightened. Yet, Athu was going into deep concentration and she did not try to distract him.

"You shall not die, Urdus!" The Shemite's words were like an incantation as he glared at the giant Vanir amid the furious melee of swordplay. "No, not now—for I will be your executioner. No sword-stroke shall slay you, Urdus, for I will save you for a later day, when your spirit will be drawn from you by painful and gigantic sorcery!"

Athu concentrated—and as Urdus fought Sonja and Thobis, the giant's sword seemed to do its work too well. Sonja's moves, faultless, nevertheless seemed to be deflected at each crucial instant by some unskilled treachery of Urdus' blade.

Now the battle was waning. Already a number of Urdus' men were running, chased by Aquilonian troops. Many headed for cover towards the cliffside, just to the south of where Athu and Aleil were hidden; they broke madly into the fringing woods, crashing through saplings and underbrush. Thobis' soldiers gave pursuit. The clank of swordplay rang from the trees, and then a number of screams—long, drawn-out, then cut short abruptly as if at the bottom of a pit.

The waterfall and the pool below! The Aquilonians were forcing the renegades back against the stream-bank, where the rogues were then being thrown back into the water to die in the thundering plunge down the falls.

Urdus, at the last moment, broke free, his magic-charged blade wounding Thobis and snaking aside Sonja's. Thobis, recoiling, stumbled into her, and that momentary advantage was enough to give Urdus his freedom.

"Into the forest!" he screamed, running for cover.

Perhaps two dozen of his men yet survived; in ones and twos they broke from the Aquilonians to follow their commander into the brush. One or two died in the escape; but Thobis did not order his men to pursue.

"Let them go!" he yelled. "We can track them down. In a day this forest will be crawling with guards!"

Then he turned his attention to the captives. Hubarthis, Desmos, Sonja and six others yet remained alive. And the great bulk of Thobis' troop. Those who had chased the convicts to the waterfall returned, wiping their swords.

Many, exhausted, sat down upon the ground, away from the bloody corpses which were already drawing flies.

"Some of you men—drag the bodies to the waterfall, and throw them in," Thobis ordered. "We have ample water," he said, turning to Hubarthis, "the streams up here are clear, but if those dogs try to get refreshment below, I want the water tainted with blood."

Desmos collapsed on a log. He had received a wound from his brother—a cut along his right side—but he had wounded him also with a slice on the cheek. Betos had fled with the rest.

"You did well," Sonja told him, sitting down beside him. She reached for a bladder of water proffered by one of Thobis' men.

But Desmos replied not at all.

As the soldiers dragged the corpses clear, Thobis ordered others to tend the wounded. One man dressed Hubarthis' scarred limbs and chest with a salve and bandages, while the Commander and Thobis conversed.

Thobis expressed joy to find Hubarthis alive, and Hubarthis explained—militarily, almost coldly—all that had occurred since his leave-taking from the fort. Both speculated upon Urdus and his band, and where the rogues might hole up now.

"Lieutenant Lobor should have turned his ship about by now," said Thobis. "We expect him to show sail to-day or tomorrow. But do we need reinforcements? We've routed the criminals, beaten them soundly, and as long as they stay close to shore we should have little problem tracking them."

"We'll get them," Hubarthis said. "They'll no longer live in exile, to plot other escapes. Death is the only fit punishment for them now. We'll dangle every one of their heads from the fort!"

"Aye, Commander. Mitra, but we'd given you up for dead!"

"Not yet," said Hubarthis, finding his new freedom heady. "No, not yet—not with such a company behind me!" He laughed.

And Thobis, for no reason whatsoever, thought back to his wife. He had not died fighting against Urdus, though the giant still roamed free.

Athu and Aleil went away, moving quickly and quietly down the cliffside toward the cave that was the eye of Swordskull.

"Aren't you worried about them?" Aleil asked anxiously.

"The Aquilonians?" Athu shook his head. "My battle is not yet with them. I want Urdus."

They continued quietly, Aleil privately worried as she followed Athu down the ravine.

They came to the pool.

Standing there at the edge of the forest, they watched as the corpses of Aquilonian and renegade alike floated in the surface, were pushed under by the torrent only to bob up again farther on and float slowly, leaking blood, some with drawn faces staring skyward in mute pain or surprise—with the sky, forest-filled and radiant with sunlight, giving no answers.

Athu laughed. Aleil started, fearful at the tone of his mirth.

On the plateau, even Sonja and Hubarthis and Desmos heard the distant laughter.

Athu laughed—viciously, evilly—the laughter of a demon seeing how his plotted course so wonderfully follows its route.

Aleil fell back as Athu's wild glee boomed out and rose to ever higher pitches of uncontrolled madness. The wizard threw back his head, screaming with mirth, spittle flying from his beard, while the waving sunlight through the trees struck his tanned face and blew patterns across it in brilliance and shadows.

Aleil cringed. *When Hell laughs,* she remembered an old Aquilonian proverb saying, *even the gods tremble.*

Chapter 8

Dusk.

Like a hunting predator, awakening to the caress of moonlight and starlight and the blossoming scents of dying day, the Shemite moved through the forest.

He had left Aleil behind in the cave. She had protested, but she was exhausted and strained beyond the limits of her mundane endurance, and Athu had spoken with her convincingly, using subtle coaxing arguments while his trained mind worked upon hers like a soporific and left her in a mild trance. Then he had sealed the opening of the cave with an invisible barrier, and gone off.

Now he prowled the forest, floating a short distance above the ground, heading for the River Shirki and the damaged Aquilonian galley.

Otos and his handful of men were on the galley. Since leaving Urdus' band, they had stolen back to the river and spent the last of the afternoon trying to salvage the beached ship. It had proved nearly unworkable; masts were shattered, canvas torn and blown away, lines snapped, the hull battered and warped—better, almost, to be reduced to kindling than remade into a sailing boat. The small skiffs and lifeboats were gone. But Otos was convinced that his only remaining chance for escape lay in repairing the damage and sailing off, and that as quickly as possible.

As the sun dwindled and the light of day died, Otos and his men worked on. One of the men, protesting that he could work no longer without rest, went away from the others and lay down in the mid-deck, soon fell asleep. Otos cursed him.

But another man protested, and then two more.

"Go, then!" Otos yelled at them. "But if Urdus or the Aquilonians attack us, you'll have only yourselves to blame!"

"We haven't seen either of them yet," countered one of the men. "By Mitra, we can neither salvage the ship nor battle Aquilonians without rest! Give us but an hour."

All lay down to rest themselves, save Otos, who slumped against the wheel on the high poopdeck and stared at the black, ill-lit Shirki, as slow-moving and despondent as his weary soul.

None of the resting men heard Athu as he dropped quietly to the night-shrouded riverbank.

None felt his presence as the sorcerer stepped into the swampy patch of moonlit water separating shore from ship.

None moved, or called out, or even ceased snoring as Athu reached the ship's side and climbed slowly upwards the rails with no means of purchase—as if his fingertips and feet created their own adhesion with the weathered wood.

None of the fatigued renegades awoke when the sorcerer crawled, insect-like, over the rail, dropped upon the foredeck, and surveyed the gray, moonlit decks of the creaking galley.

A low wind sighed. Soft waves lapped upon the body of the ship. Tackle shifted and clanked, rope groaned, wood mewed as the wind or the rocking of the Shirki touched the galley for a moment, and passed on.

The light of the moon faded as heavy clouds rolled before its broad white disc. Darkness covered the river, the galley, the forest.

Soundless as the shadow of a ghost, Athu crept down from the foredeck, his feet barely touching the wooden stairs of the way.

A man was sleeping, sprawled against the forecastle bulkhead at the base of the stairs. Thus had he slept for hours in his exhaustion, forgetful of past battles or plans of escape. Athu's shadow passed over him and held, but he did not stir. Subtly, in his vague dreams, small sparkles and dreamy starlike faces seemed to blossom and merge in the darkness behind his eyelids: the pressure of Athu's will, lulling him into deeper slumber. The sorcerer's shadow moved; he bent down, his breath barely stirring the sleeping man's hair and beard.

His spidery fingers closed over the man's face. Thumb indenting cheek, fingers spread bonily over forehead and eyes and lips, Athu pulled.

The sleeper trembled, shuddered, then fell back into the permanent abyss, his body gone limp without a groan or a shuffle. Athu's yellow eyes burned brighter as a slippery, seeping sound pulsed between the man's face and his own fingers; a crimson nimbus, as of blood-red mist, glowed around Athu's hand. The dead man turned white, whiter, became a livid pale ghost entrapped in clay and clothes. Athu lifted his hand; the crimson mist absorbed fully into his fingers; he moved on.

There were two men asleep in the mid-deck. Athu's shadow fell upon them and his hands pressed upon their faces.

Another was sprawled against the way stairs leading to the starboard passage. Athu's shadow fell upon him, and then his hand.

Two others lay asleep together, as in a lovers' embrace, against the mizzenmast. Athu's shadow came to them, and his hands.

Otos was slumped wearily against the wheel on the poop deck, having given way to sleep despite himself. He did not hear Athu climb the way towards him, but the moon at last slid free of the gray clouds and the

Shemite's intruding shadow spilled like dark oil upon the deck. Otos sensed it, woke abruptly and spun around.

He saw phosphorescent eyes burning in a mask-like face.

"Athu!"

"Otos . . ." The voice was low, almost hissing.

"What are you doing here? Why are you—?"

Otos leaped back, pulling free his sword. He lunged—

But the influence of Athu's spectral eyes tricked him. His thrust went wide. Then the Shemite's hand clamped upon his wrist, and Otos felt a chill of supernatural strength numb his arm. The sword clattered to the boards.

Athu's other hand fastened upon Otos' face, held, and began to drain him. There was a sucking, whispering, pulsing sound, a crimson glow. Otos managed just half a garbled, shrill scream before the red darkness overcame him.

The sorcerer stole away without a shadow of a sound, his eyes luminous in the night.

Early the following morning, when Lieutenant Lobor and some of his men anchored the *Hasbul* and took a longboat to inspect the damage to the beached Aquilonian galley, it was the young third mate who pronounced the fear that had entered everyone at the sight of seven white corpses sprawled upon the decks.

"Vampires!" he hissed between his teeth, as a chill went down him and a sweat suddenly glistened on his brow and arms. "Vampires. . . ."

"It must be Lobor," Hubarthis agreed, calling down to Thobis and the others from his vantage point in a tall tree upon the plateau. "She's flying military colors, though it's damned hard to see much else through those trees."

He climbed down, scraping his boots and knees on the

rough bark. "If Urdus and his devils have seen her, they'll scatter for the interior."

"The better to take up their trail as quickly as possible," Thobis said.

Hubarthis nodded. "Split ranks," he ordered. "Thobis—take half the men and lead them south. Double-time. Stick by the river. If you come upon them, have one of your men fire a smoke-arrow into the air."

"Won't that give away our position?"

"That doesn't matter in the least, now. They know we're here. They might know that Lobor is here, as well. We've got them on the run now, and the important thing is speed, not secrecy. And keep an eye out—likely they'll have eyes posted all over the forest."

"Aye, Commander." Thobis saluted and waved to his men. Wearied, they formed ranks and followed as he entered the forest. He sent two men ahead as scouts.

As the last of Thobis' men disappeared into the underbrush, Hubarthis borrowed a bow from an archer, lit a torch-tipped arrow with flint and steel and fired it skyward. It arced widely, leaving a trail of black smoke. Hubarthis handed back the bow and waited.

After a moment, a second arrow appeared in the sky, arcing above the Skirki.

"That's it." Hubarthis nodded. "Come along. Lobor knows it's us."

Then he led his men, together with Desmos and Sonja, down from the plateau towards the river.

"Flaming arrow," Betos said, looking through the tangled foliage overhead.

"There's another," spat the man nearest him. "We'd best head quickly into the interior, Urdus."

But Urdus paid him no heed. The giant sat upon a log in the midst of the forest, elbows upon knees, chin cupped in his hands, thinking. Around him stood his men—a handful, that was all. Should they stick together, or separate and take their chances in the interior?

Maybe they should still try to take the damaged ship? No, it was too late now.

"Ymir!" Urdus wiped his sweaty brow and shivered, glowering with frustrated rage. A sudden cool wind bore down on the forest, and far away thunder boomed lowly. A storm. Could it help them? Urdus shivered again; so swiftly as to seem unnatural, his brow dewed with sweat and his hands became damp.

Betos approached him. "Urdus?"

He looked up with wide eyes. His lips felt dry.

"You look pale, Urdus." Betos reached out, pressed his palm to his chief's forehead. "You're hot."

Urdus scowled and pushed Betos away. Betos eyed some of the others. One of them asked, "Have you a fever, Urdus?"

Growling, Urdus stood up to his full height. He was indeed pale, and still shivering slightly.

"We go on," he announced. "Work as a group. You two—" he pointed "—keep an eye out. Have your bows ready. We'll follow the river—"

"The river?"

"The river!" he shouted. "It's our only chance, unless you want to sit here until they hunt us down. We'll stick to the river and circle back toward them. There's still a chance we can steal a skiff or two after dark. We'll double back. They'll never suspect it."

The men nodded. Quietly, Betos said, "All right, Urdus."

"Good. Now, come." The giant turned and led the way back northward, deeper into the forest, with the Shirki just unseen to their left. More thunder growled, still far away but drawing nearer.

Behind Urdus as he led the way, Betos and the others eyed one another cautiously and formed the word with their lips: *fever*.

Midmorning, and with it, rain.

A warm thunderstorm passed, bringing in its wake a

drizzle that would linger all day.

Athu sat at the mouth of the cave, staring out of the eye of Swordskull at the mist. Aleil sat behind him, wondering.

"We will begin now," Athu said. "The rain will make the soil damp and workable. You will aid me."

"Your magic?"

Athu nodded. He stood up, still looking at the rain, listening to the thunder, watching as heat lightning played above the treetops all around. Aleil rose, approached the wizard from behind and put a hand to his shoulder. He did not shake it away.

"Will you tell me now what the clay-work is?"

He turned. She removed her hand. "Come," he said.

Athu led her deeper into the cave, which expanded into a large chamber farther in. Against one wall the sorcerer had placed his cedar-wood box and his growing pile of earth. Now he bent down and began to arrange the damp earth upon the floor of the cave. He adjusted the lines of clay, bent to scoop more from the pile, added to the outline he was forming, repeatedly collected and deposited and formed more.

Aleil kneeled to help him, but Athu told her, "I will do it. I want you to gather wet earth for me."

She stood up and continued to watch, stepping back as Athu moved around the floor, outlining a humanoid shape three times the size of even the largest man.

"This is it?"

Athu wiped sweat from his brow, paused before gathering more earth. "Have you ever heard of the Othalus?"

Her brow creased. She searched her memory. "A legend . . . ?"

"No legend. A sorcerous creation." Athu smiled and took up more earth, bent to his task. "A figure made of earth, of the clay of the world, and by certain magical processes brought to life. An Othalus." He seemed to savor the word. "The wizards of my ancient race were able to create them as they pleased; to use as servants, or warriors, or guards—for many purposes were they created to serve the Shemite sorcerers. The art has not been lost. I am even now using the process for my own benefit—and for the benefit of the one I serve." He stood up again, scraping drying dirt from his hands. "The Othalus must have a soul in order to be brought to life," he continued. "In ancient times, the souls of criminals or captured warriors were used. After a time, artificial souls were produced, though that secret has been lost; they were grown like plants, I believe. But a soul is needed. Imagine," he came closer to her, looked at her wide dark eyes, her bronze skin damp with sweat and drizzle; she swallowed, and her lips parted as if in ardor or wonder "—imagine what I could do if I possessed a body such as this."

Lightning crackled not far off, and thunder boomed.

Aleil smiled nervously; she gestured toward the clay-work. "You? In that?"

"It shall be done!" He turned again to his pile of earth.

Aleil shook her head, her face pale.

"More!" Athu commanded her. "Go, now—gather me more earth. I will be great—huge!"

She turned and walked away, came to the mouth of the cave and looked out. The landscape was gray and wet, the rain oozing down. There was no sign of sun above the blowing green fronds and trees, only gray black clouds everywhere.

"Go, Aleil!"

She stepped outside. The rain wet her hair, her limbs, her face. She clambered to the base of the cliff and headed towards the pool, where the clay soil would be reduced to mud, mingling with the loam of the forest, fragrant and rich and alive.

Aleil stepped into the soft soil of the pool's margin; her bare feet sank to the ankles in it. She removed her vest, and then her skirt and was naked to the warm rain and the warm breezes, so that she could carry the earth up to the cave.

She began to dig, tearing up rich piles of earth—soft, bubbling and dripping with fresh rain and life. Her hands felt vital and healthy as they sank into the warm, wet earth. She brought a handful of it to her face, smelled it, even licked it with the tip of her tongue; this sweet earth, this soil of life. She spread some of it upon her breasts, knelt forward so that the wet earth swallowed her knees and shins, caressed her thighs. The soil felt like a lover's body, enclosing her rapturously.

Aleil threw herself back, so that her face welcomed the rain, so that the rain spilled in rivulets from the foliage to patter upon her face and limbs and body. She nestled farther into the wet earth, and laughed, spreading her arms, spreading her naked legs, moving herself down into its warm and soft embrace.

Lightning hissed and crackled high above. Aleil laughed.

Thunder boomed. She laughed again.

She heard Athu calling to her from the mouth of the cave, his voice harsh above the slashing sounds of rain striking the mud, the sucking sounds of the earth welcoming her body.

She laughed more loudly. The thunder boomed again, the rain fell harder. The Shemite called to her once more —and Aleil felt that somehow she was magically making love to him.

"You are a strange woman," Hubarthis said to Sonja as they made their way through the dripping forest towards the riverbank.

"Not so strange. Just another sword for hire."

"You are the equal of any man."

"Better than most, at least."

They were walking at the fore of Hubarthis' company, Desmos lagging behind. As he heard their conversation —heard them speaking, but not the distinct words they said—a ripple of quiet jealousy went through him. He knew he would never have Sonja—knew that no man would ever have her. Yet he knew also that he now depended upon her in a strange, fateful way; and if Hubarthis took Sonja from him, even for a moment's conversation, then wither would Desmos?

I am not free, he thought. *I have never been free— something has always managed me. Things—impersonal forces—have always directed me, and when one has let go another has always moved in agreeably to take its place. . . .*

Whence came you, Sonja? Who are you, strange woman with a sword? Where did you learn to fight, and why do you seem like more than either a man or woman should be?

"I am not free," Sonja was telling Hubarthis. "I am driven by a strange destiny that possesses my soul and drives me to roam aimlessly over the earth."

"You must be guarded by some spirit. I'm glad to be in your company if the immortals look so carefully after you." *Where did she come from?* he wondered. *Who is she, and why?*

They came to the riverbank, close by the *Hasbul* and the wreckage of Hubarthis' galley. Lobor and several of his men were ashore and were overjoyed to greet them.

"Get aboard the skiff," said Lobor. "We'll run aboard the *Hasbul* and you can all dry out, get some hot food and tend to your wounds."

Hubarthis shook his head. "It'll waste time—"

"I've sent skiffs in both directions," said Lieutenant Lobor. "They'll send two or three men at a time into the forest to look for signs of the criminals. Never fear, they can't go far. We'll get them. Mitra!—don't argue with me. Come aboard for an hour, at least, to dry out and have a meal!"

Hubarthis smiled, and his men laughed. Sonja and Desmos were more than agreeable to the prospect.

In the skiff, Lobor confided to Hubarthis, "We found corpses on the wrecked galley."

"Corpses?"

"Drained dry of blood, but no wounds. The men fear that vampires—"

Hubarthis shook his head. Sonja overheard; she moved closer.

"It's all right," Hubarthis told Lobor. "What did the men look like?"

Lobor described them, and Hubarthis' guess was confirmed: Otos and his splinter band of outlaws. But— drained dry of blood?

"Athu," Sonja said uneasily.

Lobor looked at her, and then Hubarthis nodded wearily.

"A Shemite," Sonja explained to Lobor. "A wizard. He's up to some kind of sorcery. He uses blood."

"Mitra's heart!"

"He's still somewhere around here. He has a grudge against Urdus—or so we heard him say. I don't know what kind of sorcery he's working, but it's powerful— and it demands human blood."

The man ran swiftly through the forest, brushing past hanging limbs and leaping through thick underbrush with the agility of a goat. Past his eyes flashed the wild, blurring brilliances of sunlight and dark-shadowed forest. Years of life upon the wild Isle, stalking, hunting, had lent him the instincts of a forest animal.

He chirruped like a bird as he approached Urdus' band.

Urdus held up a hand and his men paused. The runner emerged from the brush and approached them breathlessly. He held up a hand and spread his fingers; a group behind them, to the southeast. He walked around in a wide circle, gulping in air, holding his aching sides.

"Soldiers!" he gasped. "They've struck our trail—"

"Bows," Urdus said. "Every man who has a bow uses it. Up into the trees. We'll wait for them to come this way. No one fires until we see every man of them, understood?"

The men nodded.

"Up, then!"

They took to the trees, climbing swiftly, using knotholes and branches and hanging vines for purchase. Urdus himself climbed a thick oak, and slipped twice as dizziness possessed him; there was a ringing in his ears and dryness in his mouth. He cursed at the thought that fever might be taking hold of him, then dismissed it. More likely his slowness and slight loss of coordination were due to exhaustion and smaller portions of food than he was used to.

Or perhaps it was due to the wizard.

To Athu.

Who knew what deviltry that Shemite was capable of?

Breathing hard, Urdus perched himself in the crotch of a wide, long limb. He pulled free his bow, notched a shaft and rested. Around him, at his height or sitting even higher, were his men, well-hidden by the shadows of the foliage—his men, in ones and twos, waiting vigilantly, strung out in a long line flanking the semi-natural path that led beneath them, from the face of Swordskull to the jaws of Hell.

Major Thobis heard a bird chirp in the distance. For a moment it surprised him; he had heard few birds in this forest, and it seemed odd that such a natural sound should strike him as peculiar.

But the thought of birds in the forest took him back to Tarantia for a moment, to his father's villa outside the city, where he and his wife had spent many pleasant evenings in the days before they had married.

And that thought brought Thobis to curse his abandonment in this forsaken forest, away from civilization.

Behind him his troop were making too much noise, it seemed to Thobis, for soldiers following the recent track of renegade convicts. He heard some of the men whispering among themselves; one laughed rudely, as at a gutter-joke. Thobis' lips pressed together; he turned to scold the men to silence.

As he pivoted, another bird cried out.

Peripherally, he saw a brilliant shaft of light dart at him—a bright wink of motion through a sunbeam. He heard a sound, felt a sharp blow upon his back. Then he was pushed gently forward, and as his head jerked down he saw the tip of an arrow and part of the shaft jutting from his chest, just below the rib cage.

He stared in wonder at it. Within that brief instant it struck him as strange that he should hear the sound before he felt the pain.

Time seemed incredibly slowed. He saw the first gouts of blood rip free from his chest and float like crimson pellets in the air, high above the microscopic world of mulch and moss that formed the forest floor.

Then he felt the pain.

At first dull, the pain grew and became dazzling, spreading frantically through him like some living thing vainly seeking escape. It seemed to burn outward from his chest to his head and limbs, to well up in his lungs and erupt from his throat in a shrill, gurgling scream.

His scream was echoed all around him from the forest which he could no longer see, by all his men. Thobis heard them screaming, heard the sounds of more arrows thudding home, felt the pain before his men did because he was already familiar with it.

He fell forward. The world was turning black, save for the center of his field of vision which focussed on the forest floor that jumped at him.

From very far away Thobis heard someone cry out, "The arrow! Fire the arrow!"

Yes, Thobis thought, angry with himself for not thinking of it first. *Fire the smoke-arrow! Let Hubarthis know!*

But he did not see the arrow arc skyward, launched by a dying man's bow. He saw only a small part of the forest floor, a dead brown leaf with three drops of water on it. The leaf was so close to him that it seemed almost to brush his pupil, yet was perfectly in focus.

Now the leaf was turning black. Two of the water droplets blurred.

Thobis didn't hear the birds, but a bright fragrance came to him. The smell of the earth. The smell of his father's villa.

The smell of his wife.

He choked. He saw his wife in the water droplet. She was smiling at him, the way she had smiled before they were married. Again he choked, as blood drooled from his mouth and the pain in him began to tighten in bands, suffocating him. The last water droplet darkened, dimmed—

Thobis dried to move—could not. He began to cry.

—dimmed—

He saw his wife fade, screamed at her.

—dimmed—darkened . . .

The smoke arrow sped far above the trees that hid Urdus and his band, arced against the cloudy skies, cometed towards the earth.

Sonja spotted the arrow first, trailing high in the sky, dipping earthward.

"Mark the spot," Hubarthis called out.

"Quickly," Lobor called to his oarsmen. "Turn about! Row quickly!"

Desmos looked at Sonja; there was something intense deep in his eyes.

She nodded.

Evening.

By the light of torches Athu finished his work: a giant of clay more massive than three of the largest men. It was humanoid in shape, with a gross, half-formed head that grew from the shoulders without a trace of a neck. Mere indentations served for eyes and mouth, for the Othalus would actually have no need for eyes or mouth.

Dripping sweat, Athu stood above it, dried clay and earth flaking from his hands, the flaming aura of torches playing upon his body like a reflection of Hell.

Aleil lay watching him upon a cot of straw and twigs. She was naked. Her clothes, washed in the rain, were drying upon rocks warmed by the fire-pit farther back in the cave.

She made a sound, deliberately sensual.

Athu looked at her. His teeth showed, his nostrils flared. Aleil laughed and held out her arms to him.

The sorcerer went to her. Aleil sat up and embraced him, and Athu held her. He kissed her. She smelled like the earth, like his Othalus. He rubbed his hands through her hair, his hands with dried earth on them, and Aleil gurgled and licked her lips.

She lay back, stretching, giving herself to him. Athu kissed her throat, her eyes, her mouth. He filled his hands with her full breasts. He kissed her stomach, kissed her hair, and Aleil laughed madly and brought Athu's fingers to her mouth and kissed them, licked them.

And as they made love, celebrating with one another, totally selfish with one another, the Othalus lay, not yet alive, filling up the floor of the cave. In the wavering torchlight the piled, packed earth of its body seemed to quiver and ripple, almost as if it were breathing faintly.

Chapter 9

Night.

In the light of hissing torches the tableau stretched before them, the forest clogged with Aquilonian corpses, sprawled and fallen, bent and huddled, all with arrows transfixing their bodies.

The buzz of swarming insects was loud even above the wind whipping the leaves high overhead. Already they crawled upon the bodies in crowds and fastened upon out-stretched arms and staring, open mouthed faces. Hubarthis saw a large, many-legged thing slowly making its way up the still side of Thobis' face, crawling into his thick, fallen hair.

"Urdus," Desmos said, an angry quiver to his voice.

No one replied. Sonja scowled, scanning the shadowed brush, clenching her sword-pommel.

"Bury them," Hubarthis commanded. "Now."

His men took their swords, began plowing up a section of the forest floor. Hubarthis ordered others to begin removing boulders and rocks. The night, heavy and muggy, hung thickly in the forest, tangible. A drizzle came down, slow and easy, spattering the broad leaves and thick roots. The torches sputtered.

Desmos and Sonja helped dig the trenches for the bodies. When the torches had burned low and the moon, almost invisible behind the thinning clouds, was high, the corpses of Thobis and his men were laid to their final rest, the earth pushed over atop them, and the trenches covered over with rocks. The graves were not marked.

Hubarthis led his troops in the ceremony that would commit the dead souls to the right hand of Mitra in the earth beyond this earth. Sonja, unfamiliar with the ritual, and uncomfortable around any ostentation of religious faith, stood back. So also did Desmos, for while he was Aquilonian, he did not feel it in his heart to join in the observance.

His heart was darkened with wishes for murder and memories of death, by the desire for vengeance against his brother. How could he praise Mitra and the supposedly all-seeing gods with such things in his heart?

The drizzle continued intermittantly, dampening the rocks on the graves, whispering and gurgling in the moist, fecund soil beneath their feet.

"For we know that life is an eternal combat," Hubarthis intoned somberly. "Yet we know also, O Mitra, that your sword has pierced the hearts of these men with your salvation. As the world changes from day to night to day, one thing for all time yet changing its face forever, thus have these men forsaken the body of the day for the great shroud of the unending night. They have changed their outward face, but still are they of the great All that forever is."

The troops chorused, "Still are they of the All that is."

"Lo, life is an eternal combat, but the spark of spirit in all men overcomes the fears of life and death, strips the mask of darkness from the light of eternity, transforms terror to love and surety, and makes of evil a laughing, harmless thing. Thus is the faith in Mitra, the all-seeing, whose sword is the heart of man and whose strength is the strength of men who believe."

"The strength of all men who believe."

"Return to the earth, men of earth, and let your souls fly to the clouds of Mitra. Open your eyes to the soul of Mitra, and see now what we will one day see, know what we will one day know."

"Live on as we will one day live on."

"Ius in Mitra, tento as ilsos, fethren."

"Ius in Mitra, fethren. . . ."

When it was done, Hubarthis told his men, "Turn about. We'll head north, after Urdus and his dogs."

"North?" Desmos shook his head. "Surely they'll not now return in the direction where they're sure we'll catch up to them?"

"North," Hubarthis insisted. "Look you." He took up a torch and stepped ahead a few paces, showed Desmos where faint bootmarks were revealed in the damp soil. "They were already doubling back. It strikes me that they'll return to the clifftop camp where they held us prisoner. Perhaps Urdus is hoping to lead us on a pointless chase, then try to circle back and steal a skiff from the damaged galley."

"Then you think our approach scared them away from the river, back into the interior?" said Desmos.

"Aye."

His argument did not sway all the men. But Sonja said, "I agree with Hubarthis. We can't lose much time if we follow the rogues. Lobor's forces at the river can watch the damaged galley closely. If Urdus and his men did run off into the forest again, we'll soon catch up to them. I've a hunch Urdus *is* going around in circles to throw us off, like hunted wolves sometimes do. But his circlings will always be with that galley in mind, believe me! He knows we'll get him if he remains on Os Harku."

Her endorsement of Hubarthis' plan seemed reasonable to most of the soldiers.

"We go back north, then," Hubarthis commanded. "And keep your shields ready. Did you notice the fall of those arrows?"

Sonja nodded and gestured aloft. Desmos glanced upward.

"From above," Hubarthis told his troops. "Urdus and his dogs were sitting in the trees when Thobis and his men walked right beneath them into the trap. So keep alert!"

With that warning in their ears, the men—tired, frightened, wary—headed northeast, towards the cliffs and the waterfall and the pool, and (some of them feared) death and Hell.

In his dream, Urdus was running, trying to escape something monstrous, a dragon or an adder or python grown gigantic. The serpent-thing had the Shemite's eyes, baleful and unblinking. In his fear he cried out, cursing Athu's name. The thing pursuing him hissed and opened its jaws wide, clamped them shut and then slithered after him quickly, knocking away trees and bushes when Urdus tried to hide behind them. Urdus drew his sword, stood his ground and swung, but even when he was able to pierce the giant serpent's scaly hide, neither blood nor ichor bled from the thing, but glowing, blood-red mist which collected in a small cedar-wood box the serpent carried on its back, held by two human hands which grew out from the scales . . .

"More covers," Betos called, and another man stripped off his tunic to add to the pile already lying atop the giant.

Betos ran a hand over the fevered forehead; his fingers came away wet and slick with sweat. Urdus' teeth chattered like shaken gaming-bones; his head lolled from side to side; his hands and feet jumped with the spasms of his fever.

Kneeling beside his chief, Betos bent low over him and muttered a prayer to Mitra. A man came up behind him, and in a low tone voiced the obvious concern.

"Is he dying?"

"He may live," Betos replied, wiping spit from the corners of Urdus' mouth.

"And in the meantime he holds us here, with the Aquilonians upon our trail."

"He will live."

"He may die."

Betos stood up, turned and said furiously, "Would

you have us leave him for those dogs? Would you take a vote to see how many wish to leave him for the Aquilonians?"

"We can kill him mercifully."

Betos' fingers twitched near his sword-hilt. "And I could kill you *un*mercifully, dog! Shall we abandon him when he is the one who fought us all free?"

"We are not yet free—far from it. And you are sentimental, Betos. Urdus would not approve."

In his dream, Urdus was on fire, running and gasping, a fire in his lungs which burnt the more fiercely the more he sought to escape. The large hisses and rolling, thunderous sounds of the serpent behind him prodded him on. He cast fearful glances behind, but could see only the serpent's eyes bearing down upon him. His breathing became clogged; his sweat seemed to fill in his pores and suffocate him. The huge jaws spilled rank air upon him, drowning him. He continued to run, run, yet he was entrapped in the very air, which was turning mushy, holding him back. He could not push through, he was suffocating, dying, and nothing could help him. The sorcerer's jaws would swallow him whole. He lashed out, screamed, turned and held up his sword and there was nothing there but himself, and the clogged air, and the fear, the fear which was as real as the odors in the air, the sickly stench of venomous breath still clinging to the foliage, dripping from rain-drenched leaves, softening the mossy mud underfoot.

The moon was shining down amid the dripping leaves.

"He's quieting," Betos said.

Some of the men muttered.

"Put him on a stretcher," one said. "We can lash some poles together and tie our shirts to it, carry him that way. At least we'll be making speed and not waiting for the Aquilonians to catch and behead us."

Betos seemed to ponder it.

A rough hand came down and grabbed his neck,

pulled him back. Betos fought the man off, stood up and glared into savage, fear-filled eyes.

"Don't you want to be free, Betos?" snarled the renegade. "Do you want to die in this stinking forest like the rest of those fools?"

The moon was high and enough light made its way through the heavy foliage above to illumine every face gathered around. Betos looked at all of them.

"Well?"

"We're for it," answered a few voices.

"He's past the worst of it."

"Carrying him in a litter won't jeopardize his life."

"And we have to look after ourselves."

Betos was forced to agree with the reasonableness of it. "Very well."

The men sighed heavily. A number began hacking away at saplings and stripping them; then they tied together their tunics and lashed them by the sleeves and with vines to the sapling poles. They hoisted Urdus onto the contrivance, and four men took hold of it. Betos walked alongside, wiping their chief's damp forehead with a soggy rag.

Athu stood, silent, above the trench-graves of the fallen Aquilonians, his eyes glowing in the blackness. Death could not be concealed from him, neither by forest murk nor piled earth; its presence was now a thing he felt as by a sixth sense.

As for life, that was another thing. Even before Os Harku he had felt his humanity waning as he studied sorcery more and more deeply; now he sensed life as almost an alien and revolting thing, and knew that that feeling would deepen. Even the pleasures he could still feel seemed somehow trivial, disgusting and corrupt—so he had learned that evening.

He put the thought from his mind, set down his cedar box and opened its lid. The red glow from within limned his features.

"Another sacrifice unto thee, O mighty Ordru," he muttered. "Another gathering of the blood-essence from the newly slain. *Nya ka nokomis, iantu retlaik. . . .*"

A red seepage, like a gathering of fireflies, began to glow upon the damp earth over the graves. Slowly, the crimson points of light grew, spread and began to coalesce.

"*Intu nakara, nopis Ordru anoka. . . .*"

Narrow streams of glowing crimson grew upward, twined together, then flowed slowly into the cedar-wood box. The scarlet luminescence within became brighter, almost like the interior of an oven. Then the last tendrils of red detached themselves from the ground, flowed into the box and merged with the crimson glow. Athu closed the lid; the forest instantly seemed by contrast as dark as the inside of a coffin.

But not to Athu's yellow eyes, which saw in darkness better than by day. Tucking the box under his arm once more, he lofted slowly into the air and drifted northward among the tree boles, back toward the rocky face of Swordskull.

Slowly he floated upward under the moon, beside the narrow waterfall, and entered his cave.

Aleil was asleep. Athu stood quietly and stared down at her. He bent over her and passed his hand lightly over her face.

Barely touching her, he sent her into a trance.

"You will aid me, Aleil," Athu whispered to her sleeping face. "Now the time has come for you to help me in a great way. The Othalus is complete, save for the soul. So my vengeance nears its completion. But you must help."

As if in answer to a beckoning from the lower levels of the sorcerer's vigilant mind, a sparrow fluttered near the mouth of the cave in the first gray light of dawn. It landed and hobbled on spindly legs, jerking its head here and there, eyeing the sorcerer and the sleeping woman.

Athu smiled.

"Go to the bird," he whispered to Aleil. "It will share its soul with you. Go to the bird."

He made another pass over her body, then flung his right hand towards the bird, as if flicking water from his fingers. The bird chirped and fell forward, fluttered its wings and got up.

Athu smiled again.

"You understand me, Aleil?"

The sparrow chirped and flew around the cave, flapped and landed delicately upon the sleeping Aleil's body.

"Fly forth," Athu told her. "Fly forth and discover Urdus. See where he is, and return here. Tell me. I would know where our giant Vanir is. We must prepare ourselves."

The sparrow chirruped again and flew forth, out of the cave and into the first dull light of dawn. Athu went to the mouth of the cave to see it; but by the time he stepped outside, the bird was gone, hidden in the tangle of the thick forest.

The first full light of dawn spread its warm, golden glow upon Hubarthis and his company of Aquilonians, who lay sleeping and resting in a recess in the forest. The men on guard sat at their posts, hands on swords, half-exhausted. Around them ranged their comrades, sprawled or sitting, asleep or just awakening.

But Sonja could not sleep, nor could Desmos. They sat on a fallen log some distance from their compatriots —thrown together by the circumstance, but now sharing something which went beyond their difference of sex or race or temperament. They were the only two of this company who had been aboard the barge, the only two to remember the sunny days on board the *Niros,* the rich laughter of Captain Tio, the matrons and matriarchs and businessmen all dead now at the bottom of the Shirki. They were the only two to have lived through that strange calm at the very end of the storm, when they

had but just touched upon the Isle. And still they had
breath in their lungs, life in their bodies and the desire
for vengeance raw and anguished in their souls.

"I must kill him," Desmos confided to her in a grave
whisper.

"Your brother?"

"Aye." He pressed his hands together, lifted them to
his lips. "You know what I'm thinking of? No, probably
not. I'm thinking of songs and poetry, some of the
things that used to be sung in court. Those old poems of
vengeance and death, royalty and honor and justice.
They're more true than most people actually realize, do
you know that? They speak such truth, they are so
real. . ."

Sonja said, "That criminal you once told me of,
Desmos—the one you sentenced, and who unnerved you
so. Was it—?"

"Of course. Betos."

For a long moment Desmos sat brooding. "Did
you see how eagerly those men wished us dead,
Sonja? Did you see it in their eyes? And especially me.
I'm responsible for many of those men being on the Isle
in the first place—and responsible for them being here,
in this forest, with us tracking them and them tracking
us. It's so insane!"

She watched him.

"If I get through this," Desmos continued, watching
as the growing sun blossomed within pools of rain on
the forest floor, "—if I get through this, I don't think I
can go back to my old life."

"Why not? Guilt? Fear?"

"No. Remember what you told me once about a time
coming for action? Well, we're in the action now, aren't
we! Yet I'm thinking as much as ever. Like the old
poems, where the heroes go into soliloquies. Sometimes
I thought those verses were only for the poets to show
off their mastery of rhyme and meter, but it's much
deeper than that. They had an insight which the rest of

can only gain by plodding on day after day until some upheaval like this transforms us. Isn't that right?"

"Yes."

"I can't go back. I've been changed. I couldn't even repeat the prayer Hubarthis pronounced over those graves. And before, I was always the loudest voice at state funerals, chanting those prayers and answers so piously. Just as I was always so damned certain and sure of myself in courts, at fetes, on pleasure excursions . . . It's as if all those things happened to a different person."

"You speak this way now, Desmos, but you'll find your way back. You will. You're made that way. This wound will heal, become a scar, and finally a wrinkle."

"But it will always be there. I'll go to my grave with this experience. And it's not done yet." He looked at her squarely, levelly—so unlike the Desmos of those days on board the *Niros*. "We'll not see each other after this is over."

"Probably not."

"I thought I envied you, Sonja—just as I thought I envied my younger self. All is for a purpose, isn't that what they say? All that is, is for some future? Well, here's my future; I'm living it now, breathing it, speaking it. I'm here. And I can't go back to what I was—not because of guilt or fear. I'm past that. It feels like the great calm which they say comes to men just before death; yet I don't even see death ahead. Not for me. Death would be too prosaic, an anticlimax. This thing must dog my heels for a time before death takes me." He smiled, snorted, shook his head.

"No, it isn't fear, or guilt. It isn't even wisdom. Maybe it's just a taste of wisdom, enough to hold me back, make me look at myself with no regrets. No regrets. Isn't that awesome? It's incredible . . . When I look at you, and think back to my thoughts of you when I first met you, and my thoughts of you now—I'm a change-ling."

"Perhaps, Desmos. I've learned much from you."

"And I from you."

"I want you to live."

"I have no doubt that I shall. And so will you."

"Sometimes, Desmos, I think I am almost in-
vulnerable, but for no real purpose, as if the gods are
toying with me, leading me on."

Desmos smiled slightly. He held out his hand, and
Sonja took it.

"Thank you," said Desmos.

Sonja looked beyond his shoulder. "Hubàrthis is
awake. He'll be rousing the troops."

"Are you hungry?"

"Yes."

"Then let's get some fruit and meat before the rest of
those dogs eat it all . . ."

Urdus was awake, his fever broken. His men had paused
to rest. He sat up and scowled, tried to shake the memory of his wild nightmares from his cobwebbed brain.

Betos sat beside him, offering him a water-skin and
fruit. The meat was long gone.

"You had a bad fever," Betos told him.

"You stayed with me."

"Some of us were worried that the Aquilonians might
catch up to us. But we waited. The fever broke."

"I had a strange dream."

"No doubt."

"The Shemite is tormenting me, playing with me.
Where are we now?"

"Not far from the cliffs, Urdus; they're just beyond
that fringe of trees. We sighted them just before dipping down into this patch of forest."

"Good, good. We can hole up there for a while. Tell
the men to gather as much food as they can, and fill their
water skins."

He stopped suddenly, drawing back as a bird darted
low past him, nearly tangling in his hair.

Urdus tried to follow it. "A bat?"

"A bird, Urdus," said Betos. "A sparrow, I think. Look there."

The sparrow alighted on a low branch not far from them. It cocked its head towards Urdus and Betos and chirruped.

One of the renegades nearby hoisted a bow and notched an arrow, aimed. But Urdus caught sight of him and shook his head.

"Put down your bow. Don't waste the shaft. Save it for game."

"Aye, Urdus . . ."

At that, the sparrow fluttered off, heading north through the trees, soon hidden by the tangle of forest.

"Come on." Urdus stood up groggily, holding out one hand for balance. Betos took his arm but Urdus shook him off. "I'm all right. I'll lean on my sword before I'll have anyone aid me.

"North! We'll hole up and rest a few hours; then, as soon as it's dark we'll march to the river and try to steal a skiff."

Athu sat poised, cross-legged, on the floor of the cave. The sparrow returned, chirping, fluttering into the cave and landing lightly on the sleeping Aleil's breast.

Athu smiled cryptically.

The sparrow waited while the Shemite stood up and approached the sleeping woman. Athu made a sign.

The sparrow, frightened, fluttered wildly, circled the cave several times and wheeled out into the air.

Aleil sat up, shook her head and smiled weakly. "I— I had a dream," she said to Athu.

"I dreamt I was flying through the air like a bird. I *was* a bird. I even ate insects! Then I saw Urdus and Betos not far from here. Just beyond the fringe of forest to the south."

Athu laughed.

Aleil yawned. Then she looked at the sorcerer squarely. "What did you do to me?" she asked.

But Athu only smiled darkly and gathered up some fruit for her breakfast.

The sunlight fell in visible rays upon the face of Swordskull. The columns of light wavered slightly, mist-droplets slowly swirling within them. They patched a bright mosaic upon the loamy soil by the pool. The only sounds were the faint buzz of insects, the distant chir-rups of birds, the dull tumbling of the narrow waterfall from the cliffside.

Two small shrews scurried away into the forest at the first sound of bootsteps disturbing the natural setting. For long moments there came the gradually loudening footfalls of the approaching renegades. Then the brush parted; branches pulled back for a moment, were snapped and broken and bent down as Urdus and his men came through into the clearing.

The giant Vanir led the way slowly. He was somewhat stooped, his feet dragging uncertainly in the wake of his fever. After him came Betos and the others. Urdus paused at the perimeter of the clearing. He breathed cautiously, smelling the air.

His eyes roved upon the skull-like configuration of the cliffside. No one. Nothing. Why, then, did he feel like they were being watched? Surely they were safe to rest here—

"You have come."

It was the Shemite's voice. All looked around, tens-ing; it was difficult to judge from where the voice had issued.

"You have returned, then, Urdus."

Urdus looked up. The cave—the left eye of the skull.

Athu's figure appeared slowly, dramatically, half-way up the cliffside, giving face and form to the voice. He seemed taller than usual in the sunlight, dressed in his old animal-skins, his hair straggly, his eyes burning. Be-hind him, a white shadow fluttered but did not quite take shape. Aleil.

Urdus stepped ahead, drawing his great sword.

"Aye, come ahead, Urdus!" Athu lifted his hand in a gesture. "But you alone."

Urdus tilted back his head, took a stance. "What do you want?"

His men grumbled behind him, but Urdus held up a hand, ordering them to silence.

"Harken to me, Urdus. The time has come for you and me to decide things."

Urdus waited a long moment.

"Come up, Urdus."

The giant snarled but did not answer.

From behind, Betos whispered guardedly: "My chief, you have been ill with fever. Perhaps it was sorcery—"

"Silence!" Urdus roared, turning to face him. "His sorcery failed—but my steel shall not!"

Athu laughed suddenly; the sunlight, as if in response to that laughter, hastened upon the ground in swirling patches as breezes buffeted the treetops.

"Come up, Urdus!" the sorcerer called again.

Now Aleil showed herself clearly, coming up behind the Shemite from the dark interior of the cavern.

Urdus wrinkled his face. "My men come with me!"

Athu sneered and shrugged his shoulders. "As you wish. They may watch. It matters not to me."

"It is a trap!" Urdus declared.

Athu laughed again. "Look about you, Urdus. Do you fear a mere Shemite sorcerer? Even with all your men at your back?" Athu shook his head in contempt. "Is this the man who would have freed us from the Isle? You hate and fear me, Urdus, and hunger for my blood. I offer you now this opportunity, before you are all swept away by the Aquilonians."

Urdus spat on the ground. He walked ahead, gesturing to his men, all of whom fell in behind, following him a few paces distant. He came to the worn face of the cliff and sheathed his sword, began to climb, as did his renegades. Within a few moments he had heaved himself up to a ledge to the left of the skull-face, a ledge that narrowed to become the skull's cheek bone. In a very few paces he stood before the cave-mouth, his men clambering up behind him to group upon the wide ledge to the left of the skull.

The giant stepped forward.

Aleil, who had cowered far back into the cave, was cringing against one wall; Athu, however, stood boldly before Urdus in the center of the floor. A few torches stuck in the pitted rock blazed and smoked, throwing dull shadows.

And behind Athu, lying against the wall—what was it? A huge pile of mud . . . ?

Urdus bared his sword and poked the air, indicating the lumpy pile behind Athu.

"That?" The Shemite raised one eyebrow. "My claywork. It shall be the servitor of Ordru. I have fed it the souls of your men, Urdus, and the souls of many Aquilonians as well. But now it is time you and I settle our score. Come forward."

Warily, Urdus did so.

"I offer you the chance to slay me. I will give you that one chance, Urdus."

The giant stared.

"You suspect treachery?"

"What else would I expect?"

Athu laughed. "I did not think you would be so great a fool! Come. I would settle my score with you, that I might henceforth devote myself entirely to my claywork."

Urdus did not understand. He squinted, studied Aleil, looked back to Athu.

"Fool!" Athu spat. "Fool! You could not free us from the Isle. Now you have led your men astray, and the Aquilonians bay at your heels. I have taken your woman for my own. Do you know what she has done for me, Urdus? Do you know what I have made her do?"

Urdus purpled; his sword trembled. Aleil seemed to sob or groan, as if in fear.

"Fool!" Athu said again. "Have you been ill, Urdus? Have you been racked with fever? Did you have strange dreams, and did you in your dreams perhaps envision a serpent?"

"Silence," growled Urdus.

"Did a bird startle you, Urdus? Did it? Did a bird pester you this morning, after you woke from serpent-dreams?"

"*Silence!*" Urdus roared, leaping ahead with lifted sword.

Aleil shrieked. The convicts yelled and tried to run forward.

"Fool! Fool!" Athu screamed, flinging wide his arms. "Slay me by your own will!"

Urdus' sword descended in a blur.

The great sword crunched down through Athu's collarbone and chest. The wizard's head fell lopsided; blood gushed out. Nearly halved, his body flopped to the stone of the cavern in a deluge of blood.

Aleil screamed and screamed, averting her eyes, backing away, clawing her face. The renegades stood in awed silence.

Urdus stood panting, bent forward, dripping sword clenched in his right hand, blood splattered on his arms and face. He glared down upon the sorcerer's corpse.

The Shemite's last nerve twitchings fled finally from his fingers and legs.

Urdus howled wrathfully, "Come here, Aleil!"

Her voice, racked with fear as if she were near suffocation, "No! no! no!"

A hissing sound . . .

Urdus looked about. His men stood as if dazed, staring. The torches in the cave sizzled, as if a mist-laden wind had blown upon them.

Urdus turned and stared back into the cave. Something cold brought gooseflesh out on his neck and arms.

He jumped back abruptly, swiping away at what felt like cobwebs, and saw that Athu's blood was flowing away like a live thing, toward the mound of mud at the back of the cave. The hissing increased.

"Aleil!" roared Urdus.

She dropped to her knees, her kneecaps crunching on the dirt. Athu's blood glowed as it seeped into the mud-shape, but Urdus ignored it as he stepped toward the girl.

Betos screamed.

Urdus looked back, saw Betos pointing, looked again into the deeps of the cave at the mound of clay. He could ignore it no longer, for it was absorbing the last of the sorcerer's glowing blood. And it was moving.

"Ymir's axe!" he gasped.

Aleil shrieked and fainted.

Urdus, astonished, tried to swallow, to breathe, to blink, but could not. The clay moved again, and again.

"Ymir!" yelled Urdus, his voice back at last. "It's *alive!*"

It moved, coalesced, bunched more roundly—first one limb of mud, like some huge caricature of an arm thrice as big as a man's, trembling, shuddering as if with muscular reflex. Then the other arm trembled, scraped, lifted, and something like a giant paw slapped on the ground.

The head rose slowly, huge, with a gaping mouth and blank indentations where eyes should have been, providing only a horrible caricature of human features.

One of Urdus' men lost his balance in his fear, tripped backwards and slid scraping down the face of Swordskull. His shriek was cut short by a splash in the pool below.

A leg moved, another leg, and then the torso of the thing, dripping bits of mud and clay, reared up, fell back, braced itself and reared again. It sat up, continued to rise.

It stood.

For a moment it was motionless, hunched forward, its back touching the ceiling of the cave. Then its huge head turned, slung low; the huge body trembled and rippled. A huge foot moved, the leg shuddering—then the other. Its back, scraping on the ceiling of the cave, left black smears of mud on the rock.

It walked.

Urdus' men screamed and crowded back along the ledge, began to scramble frantically down the cliffside.

But Urdus, bellowing with fear and rage, lifted his sword and lunged.

Chapter 10

"Listen," Sonja hissed.

Hubarthis and his men paused; many drew steel and stood tensely, waiting.

Sonja frowned, scowled, finally shook her head. "What are those noises?"

"Some animal," Desmos conjectured.

"It's coming from the direction of Swordskull," said Hubarthis.

"Listen!" Sonja exclaimed again. "Those were screams!"

Desmos tensed. "Urdus' men?"

"I don't doubt it. By Erlik, this is Athu's doing! Hurry!"

They ran on through the forest, breaking twigs and branches, hacking their way quickly with their swords and knives.

"Athu!" Urdus screamed. "Come ahead, you—*thing!*" Defiantly he stood his ground, holding up his sword, maddened and enraged out of fear. "Come on, Athu! I know you!"

The Othalus lumbered slowly, its bulk heaving and shifting. It held its balance precariously, swaying, keeping its arms pressed to the side of the cave as it rocked. Its feet smashed or scattered the few household items of Athu's cave: the bed of straw; the animal skins; the water bladders; the empty cedarwood box clasped with bronze and copper. As the box was kicked away, Urdus noticed that no red mists glowed within it. He looked again at the monster, realized that it contained the blood —the lives of all those slain in recent days.

Uncannily, the thing made no sound. Urdus expected such a monster to bellow and roar; but the Othalus only moved in silent, awesome power, scraping along inside the cavern, forcing itself forward.

Urdus struck swiftly. His long, sharp blade, well-tested in combat, sank deeply into the leg of the clay giant, cut free in a shower of muck—but left no lasting wound, no slice. The mud simply congealed as the blade hacked through it.

Urdus swore vengefully. Again he struck, and again his sword cut through the thick mud and came free, doing no harm. Growing horror warped his features.

He backed away, nearing the edge of the cave mouth.

The Othalus was able to move freely as the cavern widened towards its mouth. Urdus, feeling the wind behind him, the vacancy of open air, renewed his attack.

The Othalus reached for him.

Urdus met the charge furiously, hacking, swiping, cutting. Close to the clay monster he became aware of its stench, which was more than the stink of wet earth or mulch. It was the smell of death, corruption, blood, murdered souls, damned souls.

Urdus cut frantically. Futilely. A huge shadow towered over him and before he could back away a huge earthen paw wrapped around him. Urdus bellowed, hacked, could not cut his way free, his giant strength useless.

He screamed frantically, suddenly afraid that he would be suffocated, that the thing would hold him pressed to the moist clay of its body until his brain and lungs burst from lack of air.

But suffocation was a greater mercy than Athu was to allow his enemy.

The stench became overpowering. It filled Urdus'

lungs until he could barely breathe. His mighty limbs braced, bulging with straining muscles, but could not save him from the arm of clay. Urdus struggled: he drove his sword to the hilt into the soft, lifeless belly; then, even the hilt was drawn in and his hand lost its grip. He beat the thing with his fists, and they sank into the mulchy body and remained stuck fast.

Warm drops of mud dripped upon Urdus' face and shoulders. The mud clung to him. He could not pull his hands free. In a frenzy he kicked at the thing, roaring and cursing, then found that he could not pull his boots free either.

He was being sucked in.

A warmth, tingling, feverish, spread down his arms, emanating from his trapped hand. He felt something sucking at his flesh, pulling at it, dissolving it.

Frantically Urdus howled and fought, to no avail. The Othalus rocked gently from side to side, walked on, pulling the Vanir's trapped body with it as it lumbered from the cave.

Urdus was in it up to his waist, clamped securely in the monster's belly, his arms trapped. His head ached near to bursting as he strained to keep his face from being pulled in.

He screamed, pulling back madly with his right arm. Part of his arm came free.

Urdus stopped breathing, numb with shock. The flesh of his arm was gone. The part which had been buried in the living mud had been stripped of meat; it was but bone.

The Othalus moved on. Urdus shrieked, struggled, pulled, writhed, bellowed. His arm, nothing but white bone, was pulled in again, up to his shoulder.

He screamed until his mouth filled with earth and mud, until he felt the strange acidic bitterness of magically animated clay suffocating him, eating his cheeks, his tongue, his teeth, dissolving his eyes, corroding his muscles, washing away his being . . .

* * *

"Tarim's blood!" Sonja swore in a tense whisper.

Behind her, Desmos, Hubarthis and the Aquilonians were all silent—silent with awe, disbelief and fear.

They were at the edge of the clearing. At the foot of the cliff Urdus' men stood, screaming and staring upward.

Half-way up the side, in the left eye of the skull, rocking just within the opening, stood the giant of clay. It was grotesquely feeling the air, waving its hands, pressing with its feet until it nearly stumbled forward and fell, then drawing back—and Urdus, or what remained of Urdus, still protruded, half-dissolved, from its torso.

"Oh, *gods!*" Desmos hissed, averting his eyes.

Hubarthis gasped. "What *is* it? What can it be?"

Sonja ran a hand through her hair, looked down, looked up again, studying the thing, forcing her memory.

"Othalus!" she exclaimed.

"What?"

"That's the name for it! It's a legend, an ancient tale of some of the Shemites—a giant of clay. Magic brings it to life. Erlik's heart! This is Athu's clay-work!"

"Look!" Desmos pointed a shaking hand.

Urdus' men screamed and backed away, ran stumbling into the center of the clearing by the south shore of the pool. The Othalus began to lumber down the cliff. Barely holding onto its balance, it crept slowly, awkwardly, holding onto rocky protrusions the size of a man, knocking down saplings, letting loose small rock-slides.

Betos, running, fell and sprawled, lost his sword—and in retrieving it, caught sight of the Aquilonians.

"Brothers! Look you!"

"Take them!" Hubarthis howled.

His men hesitated.

"Take them!" he raged. "Damn that monster—kill the criminals! No quarter! Archers!"

Men hastily stepped forward, notching shafts to their bows. One let fly. A renegade, seeing, stood frozen halfway between the monster and the Aquilonians.

The arrow caught him in the heart and dropped him instantly.

"At them!" Betos screamed. "Fight, you dogs! *Take them!*"

But the inmates bolted, fleeing in all directions. A few made it into the forest and disappeared.

Hubarthis' men charged, encircling the criminals to hold them back. Bows were thrown down, swords pulled free. Men raced wildly in the morning light, kicking up dust, slipping in the mud at the margin of the pool as beyond them, upon the skull-like face of the cliffside, came the Othalus.

Swords clashed; screams rang out.

"Let us live!"

"We can fight the thing *with* you, in Mitra's name!"

Hubarthis stood where he was, watching, a bow in his hands, with Desmos beside him. "No quarter!" he roared. "Slay them all!"

But Sonja had another target in mind. Retrieving a flung bow, she took up a quiver of arrows and nocked one, aimed for the Othalus. Quickly she loosed the shaft, then a second and a third.

All found their mark; all sank quickly and deeply, entirely, into the lumbering mountain of clay, so that not even the feathers showed. But none did any damage—no wound, no mark, no harm.

"Erlik!" Sonja threw down the bow, turned to Hubarthis. "We must destroy it!"

"Aye," Hubarthis muttered grimly, yet hesitated as he stared upon the insane scene—his soldiers and the felons fighting in the morning light, the monster beyond them, and the grim face of Swordskull looming over all.

"Hubarthis! We've got to *fight* it!"

Desmos groaned. "Look!"

The Othalus had reached the base of the cliff. Now it

plodded on with eerie deliberateness. In its path lay the arrow pierced body of the rogue Hubarthis' men had shot. The golem came on until its feet struck the dead man; it paused, then stepped on the corpse with both feet. The body began to dissolve, the flesh stripped away and then the bone, taken up into the legs of the living mountain of clay and absorbed entirely.

Desmos dropped to his knees, overcome by revulsion.

But Sonja ran forward. Hubarthis called out to her. Ignoring him, she skirted the monster widely, reached the base of the cliff and began to scale it.

The Othalus swerved in its tracks, sensing her.

Sonja climbed, hurriedly and surely.

In the clearing the last of the renegades, a dozen of them including Betos, were slowly being corralled as the Aquilonians ringed them.

Sonja made her way up, knocking loose stones as she did so. The loosed debris tumbled down, skipping and flying; several pebbles struck the monster in the back; they were absorbed harmlessly. But Sonja had an idea.

She reached a small ledge below and to the left of the cave, then turned and looked down. The Othalus was some distance beneath but trying to clamber after her; the soldiers and convicts were a compact crowd in the clearing. Sonja looked about in all directions; if she could but trigger a landslide, and bury the golem . . .

Athu's cave was a short distance away. At the mouth of the cave stood Aleil—pale, a wild light in her eyes, trembling like a leaf in a wind.

"Aleil! Aleil!" Sonja called.

She did not seem to hear. Sonja turned, saw that the Othalus had stopped trying to climb the cliff and was waddling towards the battling warriors. Quickly the Hyrkanian scaled the narrow trail across the skull's cheek bone.

Aleil apparently still did not see her. Sonja reached the ledge before the cave and pulled herself up. Below, men were screaming as the shadow of the Othalus swung over them.

Sonja stood up, ran to Aleil and grabbed her by her shoulders.

"Aleil! Tell me what it is! Tell me how to fight it!"

Aleil turned to face her; her eyes were dark and blank, her expression infantile. Was her mind gone? Sonja shuddered. Abruptly she slapped the woman across the face twice, hard.

"Tell me what it is, damn you! Is it Athu?"

Aleil giggled. "Athu? Yes. Athu. . . ."

"What can harm it? *Answer me!* Can steel hurt it?"

"Not steel. Nothing . . . It ate Urdus." Aleil shivered violently. She laughed again; tears ran down her cheeks. "Athu made me fly like a bird."

"Aleil!"

"I saw Urdus, and I was flying like a bird, and Athu did his clay-work. Do you know what he did? He had a box of blood-mist and he—"

Again Sonja slapped her, roughly, and it seemed to startle Aleil into awareness. She looked at Sonja. Then tears poured from her eyes; she gripped herself and sank to her knees, moaning.

Sonja stood above her, sword out, angry and vengeful. "Aleil! What can kill it?"

"Nothing can kill it!" she whispered. "It's Athu! He's immortal!"

"Magic! He used magic, Aleil! Can you kill it with magic?"

She gargled a coarse laugh. "I know no such magic. I'm only a hedge-witch, I know no magic. . . ."

Sonja cursed in frustration, grabbed Aleil's hair, pulled her head back so that her teary face was staring up at Sonja's.

"Tell me how to *slay* it!"

"I don't *know* how!"

"You've got to tell me, damn you!"

"It can't be killed!" Aleil shrieked, then frantically tore herself from Sonja's grasp. Sonja was left with a handful of black hair as the woman jumped forward on the precipice, rose shakily to her feet and screamed:

"Athu! Save me! Make me a bird!"

Sonja gasped.

Aleil flung herself far out. Sonja tried to grab her—
and missed. She saw the woman fall—straight down,
falling, falling. Her body struck a boulder, and Sonja
cringed. The jolt spun Aleil's body around and around;
it struck the ground just beyond the edge of the pool,
jumped a bit, then settled still.

The Othalus turned. It lumbered towards Aleil's
corpse, away from the fighting swordsmen.

Below, Hubarthis and Desmos had joined the fray.

Betos was screaming and fighting for his life. Desmos'
sword licked out for him, cut his arm and face. Next to
him another criminal went down, sworded through the
belly by Hubarthis. Betos spun away. Blood flew into
his eyes and blinded him momentarily. Madly, not car-
ing whom he struck, he slashed sightlessly, feeling the
crush and press of bodies about him.

"Don't harm him!" he heard Desmos yell out. "He's
mine!"

Then for a moment there was freedom. Betos wiped
blood from his eyes. He was in the clear, away from the
pack where the swords were still whirling, the blood still
spurting. Betos ran.

Something hit him in the back and he was thrown
forward. In that instant he glimpsed a large rock bound-
ing away from him; the size of it and the pain in his back
seemed to match. He struck the ground face down,
skidded in the dirt, and his sword flew from his fingers.

Betos shook his head, crawled forward, got up on his
hands and knees and reached for his sword.

A boot stepped onto the blade, held it down, kicked it
away. It spun silvery, flashing, into a clump of bushes.

Betos swallowed. He recognized the boots. He looked
up.

Desmos stood above him, towered above him, sword
out, his back to the sun so that its glare played like a
fiery nimbus around his features. A shadow, a tall, angry shadow with a haze of bright sunlight about it.

Betos sobbed. "Desmos?" He crawled ahead. "Save me, Desmos." He was crying.

"Brother," Desmos whispered. "You would have killed me."

"Save me, Desmos!"

Around them rang the screams and cries, the clack of swords.

"You would have slain me, brother."

"Oh, gods! Mitra! Why should we fight? That thing will—"

"You wished me dead, Betos. You would have tortured me to death. You taunted me, gloated over me."

"Don't!" His hand reached Desmos' boot, plucked at it. "Don't!"

"Would you have spared me? No, brother, and if I spared you you would soon be at my throat again. I sent you to this hellish Isle, and you hate me for it. But now I, too, have lived in this hell, and you are the demon who has taught me to hate. We are no longer the brothers we once were, we are only the demons who torture one another in Hell. Once in my pompous naivety I sent you here in the name of justice. But now, Betos, I am a more honest man. I am going to slay you in the name of revenge."

"*No!*" Betos screamed. He lunged forward at Desmos, snatching a dagger from beneath his shirt.

Desmos sidestepped and brought down the sword in a blurring arc. Even as the blade fell, Desmos felt a spirit slipping from him, the shadow of the demon of vengeance, releasing him from its relentless hold. As the sword cut through Betos' neck, sending his head jumping free on an arc of blood—as the head rolled on the ground and the blood poured out over Desmos boots— as Betos' corpse flopped twitching to the sod—

Desmos screamed.

He drew back, dropping his sword, and knelt beside his brother's corpse to hold onto it, to feel the warmth dying in the arms, to feel the pulsebeat fading, fading, as the blood runnelled out . . .

Desmos cried out his brother's name and wept. He had done what he had promised himself he would do.

As Sonja watched, horrified, the Othalus approached the cliffside and stepped upon Aleil's corpse, drawing her into its substance.

The last of the renegades went down, screaming, hacked to death in a welter of furious swordplay.

"Hubarthis!" Sonja called.

The officer looked up at the ledge to the left of Swordskull. "Get down from there!"

Desmos, too, looked up at her. He rose, wiping his blood-smeared hands on his blood-stained mail-shirt and breeches.

"Hubarthis!" Sonja yelled. "Tell your men to get back! Get away!"

"What are you doing?"

She answered him with action. Sheathing her sword, she stooped upon the ledge before the cave mouth, began picking up large stones and hurling them over the edge at the Othalus, which still stood below, feasting upon Aleil's corpse.

"Help her!" Hubarthis called to his men. "Get up there and help her!"

Seven of his soldiers, those least wearied from the battle, ran to the cliffside, carefully circumventing the Othalus, and made their way up the steep ascent to the left of Swordskull, kicking loose boulders and rocks as they climbed. The Othalus, having absorbed Aleil's body, turned and lumbered after them.

Sonja hurried along the thin ledge, breaking free huge boulders as she went, now using her sword to pry them loose. Two of Hubarthis' men reached her and aided her. One boulder more fell, then another and another. Farther down the cliff face the other Aquilonians pried loose stones as they ascended. Quickly a wide sheet of loosened rocks and debris rumbled down, sliding and sending up huge billows of dust.

Hubarthis watched intently. The Othalus was lost to

view, as for the moment were Sonja and the Aquilonians. Striding across the clearing, the officer came to Desmos, touched the man's shoulder. Desmos, who had retrieved his sword, turned to face him.

"It won't work," said Desmos, shaking his head.

"Why not, Desmos?"

"It won't work—I can feel it . . ."

A scream from the heights, and Hubarthis knew that one of his men had slipped and fallen. Now he and Desmos saw a line of men winding their way back down the cliff-face, and with them, Sonja. As they reached the ground, the huge billows of dust cleared.

The Othalus stood chest-deep in the rubble, picking up boulders and flinging them away, struggling heavily and strenuously, fighting its way clear.

Sonja and the soldiers ran to Hubarthis and Desmos.

"That won't work," Sonja gasped. "It can absorb the stones, and then eject them. But I have another idea—"

"The corpses," Desmos guessed.

Sonja nodded, wiping sweat from her grimy face. "The corpses. Listen. The thing has been brought to life by magic. Some sort of magical yet natural force may be able to undo it. It's still made of only clay and earth, no matter how huge and powerful it is. You understand?"

Desmos said, "Fire, water, earth, wind . . ."

Sonja nodded. "Line up the corpses, Hubarthis. Have your men place them in a trail, leading around the pool from here to the waterfall. If we can get the thing by the waterfall, and push it in—"

"How? How can we push it in?"

"I don't know!" Sonja exclaimed angrily. "I don't know that yet! Maybe we'll have time to—"

"Commander, it's free!" cried a soldier.

The Othalus, broken free of the rubble, was plodding across the clearing towards them.

"Get the corpses," Hubarthis ordered, "all of you—double quick! Line them up. Leave one here, place another every few yards around the pool towards the waterfall. Hurry!"

The men hastened to do it, pairs of them dragging the corpse of one of the renegades into the center of the clearing, then arranging others around the edge of the pool. One of them took hold of Betos' headless corpse and moved off.

Desmos saw it, and Hubarthis. Hubarthis' voice was grimly sympathetic. "Desmos?"

But Desmos was thinking of other things. "Fire!" he said. "Hubarthis, gather up all the arrows, especially those with torch ends."

"Can flames hurt it?" wondered Sonja.

"Who knows?" Desmos said. "It's made of earth and mud. Couldn't enough flame dry it, crack it?"

"Set fire to the forest!" Hubarthis cried.

"Dangerous," said Sonja.

"But flames *might* crumble it," Desmos persisted. "Flame on earth? Aye, we know what happens—the thing would dry up and—"

"Maybe—but we'd better get moving!"

The Othalus slowly approached the first corpse. It paused, stepped upon it and began to absorb it. Sonja, staring, whispered a curse. "Erlik! Can anything really bring it down?" She turned and started. "Hubarthis! There!"

Coming into view were Lobor and a crew from the ship, all pausing aghast as they came into the clearing and stared in horror at the Othalus. Hubarthis ran towards them.

"What is it?" cried Lobor. "What's going on? Mitra, look at that thing!"

"The sorcerer caused it," Hubarthis explained quickly. "Sorcery. We think fire will destroy it."

"Back to the camp!" Lobor ordered some of his men. "We have oil with us, jugs of it." He wiped his hands nervously. "Move! Move!"

They had forded the shallow stream that flowed from the eastern end of the pond. Despite Sonja's hopes, the thing following them did not dissolve in the water. Now they were nearing the falls.

"Is it getting larger?" Sonja called loudly, above the sound of falling water. "Or is it my imagination?"

Desmos wiped back his hair, wet and slickened by the spray. "You're right! Look at the size of it! It's growing with every body it takes into itself."

The thing was pausing now at the next-to-last corpse. For all its hugeness and strange animation, the clay giant moved slowly, knocking away saplings and trampling shrubbery as it made its way. It came down to the high, stony ledge of flat rock that formed the north bank of the pool at the point where the water tumbled from the cleft of Swordskull. A small rainbow twinkled and glowed at the foot of the falls.

Behind Sonja and Desmos, at the edge of the sunlit clearing, stood Hubarthis and Lobor and Lobor's men. The soldiers stood ready, some with tipped arrows ready to be flamed, others with skins and bladders full of oil ready to be hurled.

"It's coming for the last corpse!" Sonja called to them.

"Move in!" yelled Hubarthis. His archers ranged forward.

The Othalus paused. Slight spray from the waterfall touched it. Sonja cursed. Though the thing seemed to act with less than human intelligence, Sonja wondered if Athu's spirit inside it had guessed the plan.

"Damn!" she yelled. "Damn! Damn! Damn!"

"Ready those arrows," Hubarthis called.

Desmos stood up. "Hold your fire!"

Sonja looked to him. "Desmos, don't try—!"

"Hold your fire!" Desmos called again, and ran ahead.

"*Desmos!*"

He rushed across the clearing, toward the Othalus. The thing sensed him. Desmos slipped once on the slick flat rocks, picked himself up and ran on.

"Hold back!" Hubarthis yelled to his men.

Sonja tensed, wanting to run after the man—but what

good would it do? Could she accomplish what had to be done any better than Desmos?

Desmos paused to hack saplings from the ground, quickly stripped leaves and twigs from them, drove their sharpened points into the last bloody corpse at the edge of the waterfall, till the ends were well-coated.

The Othalus, turning towards him, moved ahead slowly.

"Athu!" screamed Desmos. "Come on, you fiend!"

He threw one of the saplings like a spear; drops of blood flickered from it. The wooden shaft drove deeply into the clay body and was quickly pulled in entirely.

"There's more!" Desmos howled. "You fiend, there's more!"

He hurled another blood-coated spear, and a third. The Othalus swallowed them, and came on. Its huge shadow blocked out the sun as it moved away from the waterfall, darkening Desmos' small figure at the base of the cliff. Desmos howled with mad rage and hurled his last spear. The exertion threw him off balance.

"Desmos!" Sonja screamed.

An archer, shaken by the suddenness of Desmos' mishap, mistakenly loosed an arrow. It sped through the air, flame-tipped, struck the Othalus and was taken in harmlessly.

Desmos fell on the slick ledge, clutching at anything for support. His hands gripped the corpse of the renegade that lay there. He held on.

The Othalus shambled forward.

Desmos felt himself sliding over the brink, toward the pool. Clawing frantically, one hand on a leg of the corpse and the other dug into the belly, he tried to pull himself up. The corpse began to drag, to slip. The stench of the Othalus filled Desmos' nose and lungs.

"Fire!" Desmos yelled as he continued to slip. "Fire, damn you!"

Chapter 11

The fire arrows sped through the air. They struck the Othalus with sharp punching sounds. Most were instantly drawn in and extinguished, but a few left small spots of flame burning on the monster's surface.

A dozen men hurled bladders full of oil; they made popping noises as they struck the Othalus and burst. Two or three of the bags broke open upon branches as they flew, spraying oil into the trees.

Instantly the Othalus was wrapped in flame. Though it made no sound, the watchers sensed consternation in its movements as it began to rock its body and wave its limbs. The flames, huge and clinging, licked skyward, brushing the foliage all around; hellish black smoke with the odor of blood and filth rose and billowed. The Othalus stood where it was, burning, raising its huge arms, rocking back and forth on its massive legs.

Dried cakes and chunks of dirt began to fall from it and shatter on the rock.

Sonja ran to Desmos. Crouched perilously on the ledge above the pool, she held with one hand to the renegade's corpse, bracing it in place with her left foot, straining with her other arm to keep hold of Desmos' hand. Desmos had a foothold, far down on the side of the wet ledge; but his toes barely balanced on it, and he had no real chance of gaining enough leverage to push himself forward.

Thick black smoke poured down upon Sonja and Desmos. The blazing heat of the flaming monster scorched them.

"Let me go!" Desmos yelled. "Sonja, let me drop. I can swim for it. Get yourself free!"

"Hold on, Desmos! I've got hold of you!"

"The water's just below me! I can land in it!"

"Your mail will pull you under! Hold on!"

But his slippery wrist was pulling free from her.

"More oil!" Hubarthis yelled, and his men hefted more turgid bladders, gauged the distance and hurled them.

The fire from the Othalus began to pick up amid the trees; where the oil bags had missed and spilled there now shot up thick orange flames. Hubarthis began to wonder anxiously if the whole forest might catch fire before this was done.

"Hold! No more!"

Lobor slapped two of his men on the shoulders and ran on, through the growing inferno. The men followed. Pausing at a tall tree still untouched by the flames, Lobor began hacking with his short-sword at a long loop of vine.

"Cut!" he yelled. "Cut!"

Within instants they had cut free a long section of the vine. Lobor hastily grabbed one end of it, told his men to loop the other about their wasits. Then they hurried to Sonja.

As they ran toward the sheer rock, beneath the billowing smoke rising from the flames enveloping the Othalus, Lobor prayed to Mitra as he knotted his vine.

"Don't move!" he cried. "In Mitra's name, hold on!"

"I'm trying!"

Still Desmos was dragging free from her. "Damn you!" he cried. "Let me go!"

"I'll pull your hand off—Desmos—before I'll—let you drown!"

Lobor stooped, quickly cinched the vine about her

waist and pulled it taut. "Grab him!" he cried. "Grab him, Sonja!"

She let herself fall, trusting to Lobor. For one perilous moment she slid, unchecked, over the side of the rock; Desmos, holding himself up precariously on his foothold, saw her sliding towards him and threw up his other hand instinctively. Sonja gripped it strongly. Desmos lost his foothold, and for a heartbeat they fell together toward the churning water at the base of the falls.

Then the vine pulled tight.

"Pull!" Lobor cried to his men. "Pull! Pull them back!"

The vine scraped on the rock. Sonja felt herself being pulled up, felt the wet hard rock digging into her flesh, scraping her skin.

"Desmos! Hold on, hold—on!"

They were pulled back, slowly, until at last Sonja felt herself lying flat upon the rock ledge, and Desmos with her. Her fingers ached from holding onto his wrists.

They stood up. Lobor beckoned to them, and they hastened away from the ledge, with the thick flames of the burning Othalus behind them. Sonja pulled the vine over her head, looked behind.

"The fire—is it dying down?" she asked Lobor.

"Aye—but the thing's still alive."

The Othalus only stood there, waving its arms slowly, as the fire on its body dwindled. Its gestures seemed like those of a sorcerer performing a rite. And even as the flames enveloping it subsided, those amid the trees blazed higher.

"The whole forest will go," Desmos said.

"Evidently fire can't harm it," Sonja observed. She looked at the vine in her hands. "Follow me!" she yelled to Lobor and his men.

They skirted the burning trees and came around behind the Othalus, following the blood trail that had led it to the base of the precipice. When she came to a tree at the edge of the clearing, Sonja judged the height of a limb and threw the vine upward.

It looped over the limb. The free end came down, dangling.

"Find a log!" Sonja yelled. "A boulder, anything. We'll make a battering ram and push the damned thing into the water!"

They uprooted an old log nearby; Lobor and his two men hauled it to Sonja and they forced one end of it into the loop Lobor had fashioned; Sonja quickly fastened another loop over the other end of the log, so that it hung, suspended on both ends, from the limb.

"Get behind!" Sonja cried. "Push! Get it rocking until it gains momentum!"

They pushed at it, the five of them, stepping farther and farther back as the log gained acceleration with each drive until it swung out toward the rock ledge just a span from the burning, gesturing Othalus.

"Cut it!" Desmos yelled.

Sonja jumped back and freed her sword. "One more push!" she cried.

The log swung forward, back, the vine creaking and threatening to break loose.

"Push!"

As Lobor and his men pushed hard, a final time, Sonja brought down her blade. It sliced through the vine.

Momentum carried the log through the air; it arced toward the ground, the rotten end of it shattering into splinters as it struck the rock.

The Othalus, still flaming and gesturing, turned to face the sound of it. The log bounded loudly upon the rock, turned over in the air and struck the clay giant full on its side, knocking it off balance.

"Fall!" Sonja screamed. "Athu, damn you, fall!"

The Othalus stumbled back. The log slid sidewise and rolled upon the ground. The monster tripped upon it and dropped back.

It slipped. Lurching frantically, it teetered upon the edge of the rock. Then, incredibly, a great gash opened at the base of its head—its mouth, opening—

"ARKATU!" it boomed.

All present cried out in fear at the unearthly timbre of that voice, utterly unlike the sound of any beast. The ground trembled slightly, as if the very earth had taken part in that monstrous outcry, and in the same instant, the inferno in the surrounding forest blazed up furiously, infused with a supernatural intensity.

The log fell over, bumping and splintering. The Othalus followed—head first, arms waving heavily, huge legs still engulfed with oily flame, toppling and falling past the edge of the rock.

Sonja ran forward, followed by the others. Hubarthis howled to his men and all ran ahead.

A huge splash added to the spray around the waterfall. A leg showed briefly in the pool, an arm, and then the thing disappeared entirely in the great cloud of mist that blotted the base of the falls.

Sonja and the others watched. Watched, and waited. Long moments passed. The thing did not surface.

"We've done it!" Sonja yelled.

But now the flames were spreading rapidly, swirling in the mad rush of a sudden wind, reaching out into the clearing like almost sentient tongues of fire.

"Look!" Desmos cried. "It's spreading fast!"

"Get out of here!" Hubarthis bellowed. "All of you! Head for the ship on the double!"

Far off to the east, across a wide stretch of the Shirki, enormous flames were consuming the forest on Os Harku. From where Sonja and Desmos stood aboard the *Hasbul*, the entire island appeared to be enveloped in fire. Cataracts of flame poured upward, like monstrous fingers groping for the emerging stars; popping explosions erupted and sprayed fountains of yellow and crimson into the dusky sky. The whole island was being engulfed in fire, and burned, and would burn all night, and all day, and all night.

They stood there, Sonja, Desmos and all the others for the duration of the hot, burning dusk, until they could see nothing more than the mountain of flame in the dark, floating on the surface of the river, until they were as drenched in awe as they had been in exhaustion. Even at that distance they could feel a slight heat from the burning.

A faraway windy roar sounded; to Sonja it was one with the roaring in her blood, the ache of hunger in her stomach, the sting of her bruises and cuts. The eerie feeling came over her that Os Harku had become a fiery altar, and all life on it a sacrifice to monstrous gods.

No survivors had emerged from the inferno. The Othalus had not reappeared.

Hubarthis drew himself wearily up to full height. "Lobor, we can return to the fort now. The thing is dead."

"I wish we could know that for sure," muttered Lobor.

Desmos clenched his fists. "The other convicts—Mitra!" he said softly.

Desmos and Sonja stared at the flames for a long time, even after the Aquilonian galley had begun making its way up the river.

Desmos reached out; his hand brushed Sonja's; he held it a moment.

Sonja returned his pressure.

They stood like that for a moment, limned redly by the distant, towering flames.

Then they let go of one another, and turned wearily to make their way to their resting-places.

Sleep. Bathings. Changes of clothes. A good warm meal had comforted and revitalized them, even though taken in the altered atmosphere left in the wake of past madness, crime, sorcery . . .

It was after midnight. The moon was a full, silver orb riding a purple sky with fleet stringy clouds pursuing it like ghosts. The *Hasbul* still sailed upstream. The Isle was but a red glow beyond the horizon.

Desmos had dreamed—had awakened twice during his sleep in dripping fear, sweating in his metal anguish, crying out and staring at his moonlight-painted hands, expecting to see familiar blood on them.

But Sonja had slept the sleep of the initiated warrior, the restful sleep of those who have learned by necessity to shut out the madness of the world, sure in the knowledge that even a mad world pauses at times for respite. Still, after a few hours she, too, had awakened from disturbing dreams.

Now the two of them stood again by the rail of the Hasbul, staring at the wide Shirki, silver under the moon.

"Who could he have been, Sonja?" said Desmos. "That monstrous sorcerer, who sent so many to their doom?"

Sonja shook her head. "He must have aquired his powers while on Os Harku."

"Aye. Otherwise, the courts could never have sent him there. Yet, how could he have done so?"

"I'm sure he sold his soul to demonic powers, Desmos, probably in return for revenge."

Desmos glanced to the south, where the glare of the burning Isle still showed faintly. "And what of the Othalus?"

"I know not. Yet, I fear the world may not have seen the last of it. I have travelled widely, Desmos, and though I have never practiced sorcery, I have fought it and have heard many strange things about it. It is said than an Othalus can never die, though it may sometimes lie dormant for years, perhaps even hundreds or thousands of years. You may be sure that whatever being granted Athu his revenge and his powers will exact a heavy service from him. I fear the sorcerer has become a servitor of those beings who rule the Great Darkness —though when they shall call upon him to render service, no one can know."

Desmos shivered, though the night was not cool. "Let

us hope, then, that it will not be in our lifetimes. Too many have died already in blood and madness and fire, to glut Athu's hate and feed his dark masters with human souls."

Sonja did not answer. The glow to the south made a somber reflection in her eyes.

While Lobor slept, while Sonja and Desmos talked, Hubarthis, fighting his exhaustion with an iron will, stayed up half the night writing out reports: daily log; names, ranks, numbers of men lost in combat; circumstances of the deaths of those criminals pursued; the destruction of the prison-isle. How many of the exiles had died in that holocaust? All, surely.

The reporting officer will use the space below to report all attendant circumstances relative to this filing, and affix his name, seal and—

Hubarthis dipped his pen in the ink-gourd, wrote, scratched it out and tried again. And again.

The scraps of paper piled up. How to say it? How to report such monstrous, unbelievable happenings? *Attendant circumstances . . .* He could fill it out on separate sheets and then, when he reported to Tarantia, could decide finally whether to turn it in or destroy it, and verbally confide the "attendant circumstances" to some superior, so that those above him might decide what to put in the official record.

Hubarthis nodded at his desk. His lamp burned low, the quill slipped from his fingers and the gentle roll of the galley rocked him to slumber. He was so tired, so spent, that he had no dreams.

When they reached the outpost, the *Hasbul* made port for a day so that Commander Hubarthis could attend to routine details. He had ordered that no word of the adventure become common gossip; but his command did not take into account human nature. Very shortly every off-duty man at the fort was in the mess hall where the crews of the galleys were cornered into reliving every detail of the episode. Only those who had not truly fought and survived were loquacious enough to fill the ears of listeners with yarns. The handful of Lobor's men who had actually been at Swordskull backed away and sneaked out the side doors.

Sonja and Desmos passed the cool, sunny day walking in the compound yard, where dogs followed at their heels and troops nodded to them respectfully. They did not say much to one another.

Sonja continued up the Shirki on the *Hasbul* with Desmos and Hubarthis, although she had told them both, "I will not go with you into the court. Don't force me, Hubarthis. Tell them I was killed, or that I escaped ship. Tell them that. I refuse to be questioned."

Hubarthis was not quite certain how to take this, but Sonja was so adamant that the commander, in deference to the valiant aid she had rendered, promised that he would follow her wishes.

One afternoon, as the ship neared Tanasul, Sonja and Desmos stood at the rail and watched the sky, the waves and the other ships—merchanters and galleys and pleasure barges—that sailed past. Desmos smiled faintly.

"You intrigue me, Red Sonja."

She looked over at him, understanding. "Live on, Desmos. We each have a strange destiny to fulfill. Yours, I think, is just beginning."

In Tanasul, Hubarthis made all the arrangements for his journey to the capital in company with those of his men who had survived the ordeal. Lord Sir Desmos was to accompany him. On the docks, they bade farewell to Red Sonja.

"I admire you greatly," Hubarthis proclaimed. "Mitra go with you. I am much in your debt." There was truth behind the polished, military politeness of his words.

"Thank you, Hubarthis."

He turned and walked up the dock, spun around again before entering the wharfside crowds and saluted sharply, then went off down the street.

"Why does he do it?" Sonja asked Desmos.

"Do what?"

"Look at him—all military finesse. He's a good man, a strong man, an individual. He could easily be a free sword. Back there, on the Isle, he was a hero. He could be the master of some free company. But instead, after proving himself to himself, he returns to the city, to the councils, the lawyers, the scribes and officers. I know what he's going to go through; I've seen it done before. They'll grill him and roast him like a pig on a spit. They'll make his heroism out to be a sham. They'll try their damndest to whittle him down, to prove that he acted out of line, that he displayed poor judgement, that he did something wrong. And yet he's a strong man; he could be his own man. So why would he ever allow himself to be subjected to someone else's system? I don't understand. After what he's done, why has he willingly returned to a bureaucracy that will try to bleed the life from him, try to bring him down to its own level? Why would a man like him submit to questioning, orders, form-filling, perhaps even chastisement?"

Desmos laughed mildly. "You really hate it all, don't you?"

"What? The cities? No, I love the cities. You can be as wild and free in the cities, if you want to, as on the open plain. It's all a manner of instinct."

"I mean the rules. The discipline. The restraints."

"I never could understand it."

"Yet you're disciplined. If you weren't, you'd have been killed long ago."

"I discipline myself, Desmos. I allow no one else to."

"Come," he said. "Let's walk. I have time. I'll buy you a brew."

"Hubarthis has friends in the bureaucracy," Desmos

continued as they walked through the sunny, hot, milling avenues. "They won't whittle him down. He can stand on his own two feet and explain himself all right. But you wonder why he should stand for that, after proving to himself what he's capable of. Well, he didn't prove it to himself, Sonja. He proved it to you, maybe, and to me, but he acted as he did in the line of duty. He wouldn't be the same man if he were a free sword."

Sonja contemplated that.

"You and he," Desmos told her, "have very much in common with those renegades. You understand that; so does Hubarthis. So where does that place Hubarthis in relation to you? He's very wary of you. You play closer to the edge than he does; but if it wouldn't take much to make him a free soul, I think he understands also that it wouldn't have taken much to make him one of Urdus' men—or an Urdus, himself."

"You're right," Sonja agreed.

"That's why Hubarthis let you go your way. Or that's a big part of it. Duty required that he compell you to go with us before the tribunal of military investigation in Tarantia; but common sense told him that you might become more of a pest to him there than flies around a wounded stallion. There would be his superiors on one side, you on the other. Two sides of himself. Believe me, he'll handle himself much better if you're not there to tempt him."

Sonja laughed—then became thoughtful, in turn. "And what of you, Desmos?"

"I don't know. I'm still a minister of justice. Now I'm back in my own territory, an aristocrat again. I have blood on my hands, but that's my own problem. Sometimes, it's incredible to think how the truth, as it happened, can become so mangled when it is finally reported and set down as fact, to be filed away. As Hubarthis and I will do."

"Will you?"

"We can't tell exactly what happened. That would

lead to grave complications."

"It may lead to graver complications if you don't report it, did you consider that?"

"Yes. Yes," Desmos replied. "But we're not dealing here, Sonja, with men in the forest, sitting around a campfire, deciding how to take action to survive. We're dealing with aristocrats and bureaucrats. Different ways to save different parts of ourselves. But I know you can understand that."

"Yes, I understand. I simply want no part of it."

They came to a tavern and went inside. It was crowded with the usual motely assemblage of nationalities and classes of persons common to dockside towns. They took a table and ordered ale.

"Have you any money?" Desmos asked.

"Incredibly, yes," Sonja replied. "I still have the full purse I had when I stepped aboard the *Niros*. It was on my sword-belt."

"I just wanted to make sure. I can pay for the brew. . ."

They sipped their ale, and their conversation died away. Sonja's thoughts raced ahead. She must buy a horse, that was first. Perhaps linger in the city for a day or a week, but then move on.

She felt a need for wide space, a plain or a trail or a desert in which to work out this adventure, this latest act of fate. She finished her brew and ordered another, and a second for Desmos—then noticed that Desmos was watching her carefully.

"Take care," he told her. "Wherever you travel, take care, won't you?"

"Surely, Desmos. I wish the same to you."

"Perhaps—someday . . ."

She smiled, and gripped his hand.

When they had nearly finished their second brew, Desmos stood up and excused himself, went through the crowd to the counter and ordered two more. Returning, he found that Sonja had gone.

As he had half expected.

He whispered, "Mitra go with you, Hyrkanian. Guard yourself well . . ."

Some part of him loved her, and he knew it, and drew strength from that.

He made his way again to the table and sat down. A plump girl came by with a tray. Desmos pulled out his gold.

"For the red-haired—"

"She paid already. I see you have plenty of brew for now, advocate."

"Aye." He finished his second cup and, starting on his third, felt a pleasant strength take hold of him—the ale, perhaps—and stared at the wet ring left on the table from Sonja's cup.

The island was situated in the middle of the Shirki River. If it had ever been dubbed with an official name, that was long ago forgotten by the Aquilonian scribes, for the isle was known all along the coast by its more common and descriptive appellation: *Os Harku*, the Isle of Ill Harbor. Or, more simply, the Isle. It was not visited by merchant ships or cruising trade vessels, nor did daily galleasses from the Aquilonian forts on the shore patrol the waters about it any more. Os Harku was no longer populated, not by settlers or immigrants, not by criminals, not by any living thing. It was but an isle of cinders and scorched rock, of death and desolation. . . .

And away from Tanasul, mounted on a white stallion bought for half a purse of gold, with her sword at her side and her flaming-red hair blowing in a cool breeze, her armor glinting, her lips laughing, Red Sonja rode into the homeless steppelands and was welcomed by the old freedom.

WHY WASTE
YOUR PRECIOUS
PENNIES ON GAS OR
YOUR VALUABLE
TIME ON LINE
AT THE BOOKSTORE?

We will send you, FREE, our 28 page catalogue, filled with a wide range of Ace Science Fiction paperback titles—we've got something for every reader's pleasure.

Here's your chance to add to your personal library, with all the convenience of shopping by mail. There's no need to be without a book to enjoy—request your *free* catalogue today.

ACE SCIENCE FICTION
P.O. Box 400, Kirkwood, N.Y. 13795   A—05

WITCH WORLD SERIES

- [ ] 89705 **WITCH WORLD** $1.95
- [ ] 87875 **WEB OF THE WITCH WORLD** $1.95
- [ ] 80806 **THREE AGAINST THE WITCH WORLD** $1.95
- [ ] 87323 **WARLOCK OF THE WITCH WORLD** $2.25
- [ ] 77556 **SORCERESS OF THE WITCH WORLD** $2.50
- [ ] 94255 **YEAR OF THE UNICORN** $2.50
- [ ] 82349 **TREY OF SWORDS** $2.25
- [ ] 95491 **ZARSTHOR'S BANE** (Illustrated) $2.50

Available wherever paperbacks are sold or use this coupon.